FOREVER BETTER TOGETHER

A.D. ELLIS

INTRODUCTION

This story is part of the Common Elements Romance Project.

100 Romance Writers, 5 Story Elements.

https://commonelementsromanceproject. wordpress.com/

Each story in the project could be a romance of any sub-genre, but HAD to include the following elements:

-->a lightning storm

-->lost keys

-->a haunted house (really haunted or rumored to be)

-->a stack of thick books

-->a person named Max (which can be short for something)

These books will be releasing between October and January with tons of fun and giveaways on Facebook. Be sure to check out ALL the information at the above link.

AUTHOR'S NOTE

This story was so much fun to write! The idea for Quincy and Griffin came about from a simple text I stumbled upon between two stepbrothers. Of course, I took artistic liberties, but this entire story grew from that one text I saw. I hope you love Quincy and Griffin as much as I do.

1

QUINCY SANDERS

I GRABBED my phone from the pocket of my hoodie. Empty Chinese containers littered the coffee table as Dad and I watched a movie, but he was absorbed in his computer, and I had no idea what the movie was even about. I pulled up Griffin's number and sent him a text.

Me: *You having fun, bitch?*

Griffin: *Yeah, where are you?*

Me: *My dad's.*

Griffin: *Again? Damn, man, sorry.*

Me: *Yeah, for the week. It's not bad.*

Griffin: *Awww yeah, I get the room to myself.*

Me: *Jack off all you want.*

Griffin: *Nah, it just means I get to watch Disney movies and cry without you making fun of me.*

Me: *And jack off.*

Griffin: *Okay, and jack off.*

I snorted.

Griffin was my brother and best friend.

Okay, he wasn't my blood-related brother, but that didn't matter to me. He was my brother in all the ways that mattered. We were sixteen, but we'd known each other since we were ten. He became my brother when we were twelve.

"What are you over there snorting about?" My dad, Max, removed his glasses and looked away from his work like he really was interested. He was a great guy, and I loved him, but he had a bad habit of getting too involved in his work and forgetting his family.

"I was talking to Grif, and got to thinking about how much we clashed when he first moved in." I shook my head.

"Oh, Momma and Pops told me how terrible you guys were at first." Dad laughed. "Glad you finally decided to get along. Pretty sure Momma would have kicked both your asses if you hadn't."

"It wasn't like we *hated* each other; we just clashed. We had absolutely nothing in common and Momma threw us together and basically expected two ten-year-olds to work out their differences."

"Well, you two must have done a pretty good job since he's your best friend. Momma usually knows what she's doing."

"Yeah, she sure called it right. I never would have believed it then, but it worked out." I smiled at the thought of when I first met Griffin.

. . .

Six Years Ago

Momma, that's what everyone called my grandma, held the hand of the tiny, fragile looking boy, who was about my age.

"Quincy, this is Griffin. He's going to be staying with us for a while," Momma said. "Griffin will share your room; there's plenty of space." This was said in her no-nonsense way that meant no arguing or backtalk.

Griffin barely glanced at me, but I saw tears in his big blue eyes.

Damn it. I didn't want to come across like an asshole, and Momma would have my ass if I did. But I didn't want to share my room.

Bad enough my mom was dead and my dad was overseas building business startups for years at a time then add in the fact that my grandparents, Momma and Pops, took in foster kids and I never had any privacy. Then Momma introduces me to this kid who looked like he would faint if I said anything to him. *Damn it.*

I loved my grandparents and knew they had huge hearts to take care of those less fortunate. I just would have liked it to be in a way that didn't require me to share my room. The last time I shared my room, Momma had rolled in two cribs and I'd spent six months sleeping with babies who'd cried at every hour it seemed.

"Quincy, say hello," Momma urged and raised her brows.

"Hi, Griffin. Nice to meet you," I mumbled and held out my hand.

Griffin hid his head in my grandma's side.

"He's been through a lot. Let's get him set up in his room." Momma left no room for discussion.

Griffin and I followed her up the stairs and down the hall.

"Here we go. This is where you'll sleep. The bed is very comfortable." Momma pointed to the far side of the room where the spare bed was positioned. "The closet is huge so you both can put your clothes in there."

"I don't have no clothes anyway," Griffin mumbled.

"We'll get you all set up, sweetie," Momma assured. "Now, I've got to see about the other children and get dinner started. You boys get to know each other. I'm sure you'll be the best of friends."

Griffin stood in the middle of the room looking scared to death.

"Look, this is a nice place. Momma and Pops will take care of you." I felt the need to reassure him.

"I know you don't want me here. No one ever wants me anywhere," Griffin whispered. "I'm sorry you have to give up your room to me."

My heart hurt for the kid. But damn Momma for putting him in my room. He would have been better with the little ones. He seemed like he was scared to death of me.

Griffin was short. He likely weighed less than me by at least twenty pounds. His skin was fair; my skin was dark. His eyes were blue; my eyes were deep brown. His hair light brown; my hair black. He had a look of perpetual fear and fragileness; I was sturdy, strong, and not afraid of much.

"Nah, you keep out of my business and don't bother me, we'll be fine roommates." I plopped on my bed. Did Griffin want to tell me what brought him to Momma and Pops? Probably not. Most foster kids didn't have great stories to tell. "You got questions?"

Griffin sat gently on the side of his bed. "Are Momma and Pops your parents?"

I laughed. "Not really. They're my grandparents officially, but they might as well be my biological parents. My mom died when I was born. My dad, his name is Max, he's great. But he works in other countries setting up businesses. I've lived with Momma and Pops since I was about three. I go visit my dad any time he's back in the United States."

"What's the school like here?" Griffin whispered.

I immediately hated the thought that he'd be going to the run-down trash public school down the street. He'd either be eaten alive or he'd be such a non-threat that no one would pay him any attention. I prayed for the latter. I'd have to tell the few remaining neighborhood kids who went to the public school to keep an eye out for him.

"Well, it's not the best school ever," I hedged.

"Figures. None of the schools I've ever been to have been good." Griffin ran a hand along the comforter. "Do you at least like it a little?"

I swallowed hard and tried not to feel guilty. "Um, I

don't go to that school. A lot of kids in this area go to private schools."

Griffin's eyes were wide. "Wow, private school." He shook his head. "We are probably the most different kids to ever share a room."

I laughed. "Possibly."

"Is there a washing machine? I probably need to get these clothes washed; I've had them on for a few days." Griffin picked at a spot on his shirt.

"Momma will do your laundry. She'll get you some clothes for now. She's always got all kinds of clothes in different sizes. Then she'll probably take you shopping and get you all set up for school." I glanced around the room. "You can do your homework at the kitchen table or on your bed. Use that little table if you want." I gestured toward the small table. "I use the desk for my homework."

Griffin nodded. "I like to do homework. Keeps me busy and out of the way."

I frowned. "You *like* homework? Gross."

He shrugged.

"What else do you like?"

"I like to read and watch movies. Dancing is fun. I like makeup videos." He added that last part almost as a challenge.

"Like Halloween haunted house type makeup?"

He shrugged. "Any kind. You think that's girly?"

I shook my head. "Whatever floats your boat. Momma and Pops don't allow us to judge others for what they come from or what they like." I glanced at my collection of DVDs. "What kind of movies?"

"Mostly Disney if I can find them," Griffin said.

"I think I've got some Disney down there. I've also got a ton of movies on my computer." I got up and pulled out the laptop I used only for watching movies. "I don't use this for homework or anything. You can use it to watch movies if I'm not using it."

The way Griffin's eyes lit up made me feel guilty for being mad about sharing my room.

"You like dancing? What about singing?" I asked.

Griffin nodded but looked suspicious.

"There are two girls here who love to dance and sing and put on shows. I bet they'd be thrilled for you to do their makeup and help with dancing and singing."

Griffin didn't say anything, but I thought he looked pleased with the idea.

THE NEXT DAY, after a night of *trying* to sleep even though Griffin seemed to toss and turn, Momma came bustling into my room.

"I figure we better get you some clothes and shoes," she told Griffin as she tossed my laundry on my bed and took Griffin some clothes. "These will get you through at least today. You get a shower and change into these. Quincy, you show Griffin where the laundry goes. We'll leave for shopping after breakfast. Just the three of us."

"Momma," I began to protest but the look she shot me had me biting my tongue.

Griffin kept his head down and scurried to the bathroom across the hall. I heard Momma tell him where the towels and washcloths were. Then she tramped down the stairs as the water came on.

When Griffin came back to the room, his hair still wet, he looked like the shower had breathed new life into him. "I'm sorry you have to go shopping with us," he murmured.

"No worries. Momma will buy us lunch, so it's not all bad." I stood from the Lego set I was working on. "I'm going to shower, then it will be breakfast. You can use my Legos if you want. Just don't lose any of the pieces. And we have to be sure they are cleaned up. You don't want to see Momma if she steps on a Lego."

Griffin smiled slightly and it warmed my heart. From that point on, I promised myself I'd do everything in my power to give the kid something to smile about. He might have been intruding on my privacy, but he didn't seem to have much bringing him smiles, and I wanted to give him that.

When I came back from my shower, Griffin was on the floor putting together the bricks, but he dropped them and scooched across the floor as soon as he saw me. "Sorry, I didn't mess them up, I promise."

I shook my head. "No worries, Grif, I told you that you could play with them."

He smiled. "My mom used to call me Grif when my

dad wasn't around. He hated it. Said it made me sound like a dog or something."

"I'm sorry, would you rather I not call you Grif?"

"No, I like it."

"Cool. I've got more where that came from G, G-Man, The Griffin-nator." I laughed at Griffin's scrunched up face. "Okay, okay. Griffin, Grif, and maybe G. Nothing else."

Griffin nodded and bit back a smile.

He helped me clean up the blocks, and we headed down to breakfast.

At that point in time, Momma and Pops had two girls around five or six, a baby about two-years-old, and a baby about one-year-old, plus Griffin and me. Breakfast was a lively affair and Momma expected me to help as much as possible. Griffin sat quietly and took it all in. The friendliness, laughter, and easiness in the room seemed unfamiliar to him. When one of the girls knocked over her milk, Griffin's face immediately took on a look of shear panic. But Pops just grabbed the cup and wiped up the milk telling us all, "No need to cry over spilled milk." Griffin's eyes grew wide and he continued watching the scene before him in seemingly absolute shock.

By the time we headed out to the store, Griffin looked as if his eyes would never go back to their normal size.

"I guess this is all kinda new for you, huh?" I asked as we sat in the far back of Momma's van.

Griffin could only nod.

"Not all families are bad," I said.

He gave me a look that showed his doubt, but we arrived at the store before we could continue the conversation.

Momma marched us to the boys' section and had Griffin try on a few things.

While he was in the dressing room, which I figured was another new thing for him, I stood close to Momma. "He's not used to this."

"I reckon not," she agreed.

"You got enough for clothes and some other things?"

She side-eyed me. "I've got enough. Why?"

I shrugged. "Just thinking he'd like some stuff of his own in my room."

"We'll get shoes next, and then we can get some toys or games."

"Probably would like some books and movies," I suggested.

She gave me a look, but nodded. "We'll get him all settled. He's been through a lot."

"Yeah," I said sadly. "Think he wants to talk about it?"

"That will be up to him. Don't press him." Momma put her arm around me and pulled me close. "I know I don't usually make you share your room if I can keep from it, but I think Griffin needs to have a friend his age."

I just nodded. "Sucks he's gotta go to that crap school."

"Watch your mouth," Momma warned, but she sighed. "I hate that he has to attend Briar Ridge, but there's no way around it. We don't get enough money from the state to pay for private school tuition. We'll just have to help him as much as we can at home."

Griffin finally opened the dressing room door, and Momma and I turned around.

"Well now, you're looking quite spiffy. These sizes look right, just as I suspected." Momma fussed over Griff's pants and shirt. "We'll get a couple pairs of pants and some more shirts. Won't have to try them all on since we know these fit."

"More? One is fine, thank you," Griffin stuttered.

"Man, you can't wear one pair of pants and one shirt all week." I shook my head.

Griffin returned to the dressing room and changed out of the new clothes before returning to where Momma and I stood.

"Come on," I demanded, and we followed Momma to the shelves of pants and shirts.

Momma held a pair of khakis and a pair of jeans. "You like jeans or pants better?"

Griffin simply shook his head and whispered, "I don't know. Any are okay."

"Momma, he needs some sports pants too," I interjected. "Jeans, khakis, and two sports pants."

Momma nodded and gathered up the items I listed. "Okay, now shirts. I think we can do seven shirts. These are on a great sale."

Griffin looked as if he was about to fall over.

"Come on. Pick some colors," I urged.

When Griffin just stood and ran a hand over the shirts, I stepped in. "I think you need a blue, black, and red for sure."

Griffin just watched as I threw the shirts in Momma's cart.

"What's your favorite color?"

"Pink, red, and baby blue," Griff muttered.

"Okay, that makes it easy. Already got the red. Here's a nice pink and a baby blue." I tossed those in the cart. "You have to pick the next two by yourself."

Griffin bit his lip and looked as if he was about to hyperventilate, but he gently picked up the darker pink option and the orange. He glanced at the cart as if afraid to put the shirts in it.

"Toss 'em in," I commanded. "Shoes next, right Momma?"

"Yes sir," Momma agreed with a smirk.

I was used to pricey shoes because my dad made enough money to keep me in them. The shoe selection at this store was *not* what I was used to, but Griffin looked at the shoes as if they were the best things he'd ever seen. For the first time, I noticed his shoes and realized he probably hadn't had new shoes in a very long time, if ever.

Momma had Griffin step on the measuring tape sticker on the tile floor so we knew what size he needed.

"What do you like? Colorful? White? Black? Hi-tops or low tops?" I pointed to different shoes as I asked.

Griffin just shook his head. "Any are fine. Just would like them to not hurt my feet," he whispered.

Momma pulled Griffin close and kissed the top of his head.

I noticed he tensed up, but after a second, he leaned into her embrace. *Momma's hugs would do that to you.*

Griffin pulled away, blushing. "I've never had new shoes, so I'm not picky."

I grabbed four pairs in his size and placed them on the bench. "Start with those and see what you like."

Griffin decided on a pair of mostly white sneakers with a black logo. "It feels like there are pillows on my feet."

"Let's take a look at some books and movies before we head to lunch." Momma wiped a tear from her eye and led us toward the books and movies.

Ten minutes later, Griffin stood in awe of the movies. He held two Disney storybooks in his arms already.

"I'll just get these two books. I can get a lot of books from the library," Grif had stated while picking his two books. "I mean, if you have a library card," he stumbled over his words as if he was afraid he'd overstepped his boundaries.

"Of course, child," Momma gushed. "We'll get you one of your very own. Now, go pick a couple movies. Make 'em your favorites. You can rent all the movies you want from the library along with your books."

So, Griffin stood looking at the movies. Disney movies.

"Why you like Disney movies so much?" I picked one up and looked at the back. "I mean, I'm not against them, they just seem kinda childish."

Griffin sighed. "I guess because they give me hope. A lot of Disney movies teach lessons about not letting your past get you down, being yourself and loving yourself, not judging others, reaching for your dreams, and believing in yourself. Disney movies make me feel like there's hope for me."

"Wow," I breathed. "Okay, I can see it."

"The future isn't going to know what hit it when you're unleashed on it, baby boy," Momma assured Griffin. "Both of you, I know you're both going to do amazing things and don't ever let anyone tell you different."

Momma had Griffin and me run to the restroom while she checked out. I think she probably didn't want Griffin to see the total for all she bought him. I knew she got money from the state for caring for foster kids, but I had a feeling Momma dipped into her own personal money to cover all of what we picked up for Griffin.

Once we were in the van, Momma asked us if the local burger place was okay for lunch.

When it was obvious Griffin didn't have a clue about eating out, I told Momma it would be great for lunch.

"Are you rich?" Griffin whispered.

I thought for a moment. "*I'm* not rich. My dad is rich. He makes sure Momma and Pops have enough money for themselves and for me. So, I get nice stuff, but Momma and Pops don't spoil me. At least not usually. Like I can't just get anything because I say I want it."

"Wow." Griffin blew out a breath.

Momma whipped the van into the burger joint. "Hope you're hungry, boys! I'm starving."

The three of us trooped into the restaurant and waited to be seated.

"Whoa," Griffin whispered. "This is like a *real* restaurant?"

I gave him a look. "Yeah, it's real." I frowned.

As the hostess led us to our table, Griffin shrugged beside me. "I just never been to a real restaurant. Just fast food, mostly cold from a drive-through."

My heart wobbled between feeling so damn sorry for this kid and being so damn thrilled he'd been placed with Momma and Pops because I knew he'd get to experience all he'd missed out on and more.

Griffin seemed overwhelmed by the menu.

"You like burgers and fries?" I asked.

He nodded.

"You want to get what I'm getting? It's a double burger with cheese, fries, a milkshake, and a drink." I pointed at the meal I was going to get.

"That sounds like a lot of food. What if I can't eat it all?" Griffin worried his bottom lip.

"You can do your best," Momma assured. "And if you can't eat it, I'm sure this bottomless pit will help you finish it up."

I grinned.

In the end, Griffin ate all but about three bites of his burger and five fries. He looked to be on the verge of a food coma as he slurped the rest of his vanilla shake.

Momma paid for our meal and we headed home.

"Pops will be ready for a break from the babies," Momma joked. "Griffin, I'll get all the new clothes washed. You boys have the rest of the day to play. Tomorrow we'll make sure everything is ready for school."

I groaned about going back to school.

Griffin looked anxious, but he said, "School isn't usually that bad. It's warm, you get food, and the teachers are mostly nice."

I felt like an ass.

"Well, feel free to help me with my homework," I teased and bumped his shoulder.

Griffin nodded. "I will."

THAT NIGHT a fierce lightning storm woke me. The storm was far enough away that the thunder was still a far-away rumble, but the flashes of lightning were so bright they lit up my dark room as if the sun were shining. God, I hated lightning. Thunder was bad too, but at least thunder couldn't start a fire or kill a person like lightning could.

As I rolled over, ready to cover my head and try to sleep through my fear, I saw Griffin sitting up in bed. "Hey, you okay?"

Griffin sniffed. I knew he'd been crying even before the lightning bolt shone light into my room and revealed his tear-streaked face.

I rolled from bed and padded my socked feet over to Griffin's side. "You scared of the lightning too?"

Griffin drew his knees to his chest and wiped his eyes on the pajama bottoms Momma had thrown in the shopping cart at the last minute. "Kinda. The lightning is sort of scary when it's so bright."

"You hate the thunder?"

"Yeah, especially when it shakes the house." Griffin turned his head to look at me. "Sometimes the thunder can hide other sounds."

"Like what?"

"When my parents used to fight, I didn't mind if it thundered because it would hide the sounds of their words." Griffin shivered.

"They used to fight a lot, huh?" I sat on the edge of his bed.

Griffin sniffed again. "Fight, scream, throw things. My dad would slap and punch."

"Oh, God. That's bad. I'm sorry." Another flash of lightning was followed by a distant rumble of thunder. "Is that why you're in foster care?"

"No." Griffin shook his head and was quiet for so long I almost thought that was all he was going to say. "My dad got really mad one night. He shot my mom and then himself."

My heart clenched and my eyes stung. I reached out and touched Griffin's knee. "I'm sorry."

Griffin scrunched up his face. "I wasn't sad he was dead. But I miss my mom. She tried to be good."

"Boys, you need to be in bed." Momma appeared in the room out of nowhere.

I jumped, already spooked by the lightning storm and Griffin's story. I wondered how long Momma had been at the doorway.

"Scoot together if you want to chat until you fall asleep, but back in bed, both of you."

Griffin gave me a look that said he was ready to scoff at Momma's suggestion if I did or start pushing his bed across the room if I gave the slightest indication I was okay with it.

"You want to?" I stood.

Griffin scrambled out of bed and helped me scoot his bed across the room until it was flush with mine.

Momma gave us both a hug and kiss and told us to go to sleep.

Maybe it was having a person so close. Maybe it was the gratitude I felt in my heart that I'd never dealt with anything as scary as what Griffin had been through. Maybe I was just tired after a long day of shopping. My mind raced with what I had learned that night and how good it felt to have Griffin near and how weird it was that I'd gone from being mad about sharing my room to happy that Griffin was there.

"Grif?"

"Yeah?"

"I'm sorry you've had a pretty sucky life." I reached out and patted his hand. "But you're in a nice place now. Momma and Pops will take good care of you. And I'm your friend, no matter what. You can tell anyone that."

Griffin was quiet for a while. "I've never really had a friend."

"You've got one now."

Griffin yawned. "This *is* a nice place. I've never really had one of those either."

I squeezed his hand.

We drifted off to sleep. Our friendship had taken root.

2

GRIFFIN MURPHY-SANDERS

I STARED at the text from Quincy and smiled.

Quincy: *You having fun, bitch?*

Me: *Yeah, where are you?*

Quincy: *My dad's.*

Me: *Again? Damn, man, sorry.*

Quincy: *Yeah, for the week. It's not bad.*

Me: *Awww yeah, I get the room to myself.*

Quincy: *Jack off all you want.*

Me: *Nah, it just means I get to watch Disney movies and cry without you making fun of me.*

Quincy: *And jack off.*

Me: *Okay, and jack off.*

QUINCY SANDERS WAS MY BROTHER, my best friend, and my family.

I came to Momma and Pop's as a scrawny, scared,

traumatized ten-year-old, and Quincy took me under his wing and made the bad not so terrible.

Momma and Pop officially adopted me when I was twelve. Have to admit, never thought I'd have a true family. My childhood was shit until I met the Sanders. They turned everything around. And Quincy quickly became my protector, my supporter, my friend.

I kinda hated when Q went to see Max. I respected the fact that he loved his dad and wanted to spend time with him. In fact, if I was being honest, I was probably pretty damn jealous that he had a rich and caring, if somewhat distracted, father. But when Quincy was gone, I was lonely. The house was always full. Momma and Pop were always there for me, and I truly loved them like I never thought I'd love any adults.

My mom had tried her hardest, I really believed that. But she couldn't overcome her addictions, her demons, and her fucked up love for my dad. When he killed her and himself it left me all alone. My first couple foster homes were the absolute worst. The parents only wanted the check from the state. The kids were ignored, the houses were barely clean, and the adults were angry or uninvolved at best.

But then I was placed with Momma and Pops and all that changed.

For the first time, I was clean, clothed, fed, and safe. I was allowed to be a child. I got to play with other kids. I was allowed and expected to go to school. For the first time in my short life, I was wanted. Maybe even loved.

Two years after coming to the Sanders' house, I *knew*

I was loved when they asked me if I wanted to be theirs forever. Did I want to have Momma and Pop as my parents? Quincy as a brother? A forever home? Hell, yes.

They completely understood why I wanted to keep my last name to remember my mom; Momma didn't even blink when I asked if I could have the last name Murphy-Sanders. Explaining why I wanted to honor or remember my mom when she wasn't all that great in the first place was hard, but my heart always felt the need to keep her close. Momma, Pops, and Quincy never even questioned my decision.

Quincy and I took to being brothers somewhat easier than we took to being best friends. We did everything together, but we were and had always been, a walking contradiction. Q loved comedies and action movies; I loved Disney movies. The more they made me cry, the better. Q was thick, dark, and strong; I was thin, fair, and scrappy. Q loved Legos and sports of all kinds; I loved dancing and costumes and makeup. He had money; I had only what Momma and Pops could provide. And what they provided was more than enough and so very much appreciated. Max was beyond rich and provided for Quincy. He didn't lavish Q or spoil him. But Quincy never wanted for anything. Once I came to Momma and Pops' there was no *need* not met. But they couldn't provide my *every* want. However, I never felt like I *had* less. Q always shared and thought to include me in everything he could. But I won't lie, I often felt like I *was* less. Not because of anything Momma, Pops, or Quincy did. Just my messed-up head always telling me I'd never be Quincy's equal.

School was the only area where I felt ahead of Quincy. He complained endlessly about school; I found comfort in books and learning. School seemed to be the way out of my traumatic past. Momma and Pops had vowed to be there forever, but I couldn't rely on them to pull me free. An education was my ticket to everything I dreamed of.

The school I went to was a lot different than Quincy's. Max paid for Q to go to a fancy private school. I went to the public school in Momma and Pops' neighborhood. Since so many of the kids in their area went to private schools, the public school got very little funding from the state because it had such a small enrollment. The building was run down, most of the students came from poverty, and the teachers were overwhelmed and burned out.

But I thrived at school. Momma said I was one of the smartest and most driven kids she'd ever known, and she was excited to see how far I'd go. I soaked up anything and everything. I knew from sixth grade that if I was going to get to college, I would need scholarships. Momma and Pops assured me that we'd qualify for need-based scholarships. But I wanted to score as many academic-based scholarships as possible.

Quincy and I began plotting our college plan in middle school. We'd go to the same school. Period. Quincy would do something with sports; I'd do something with business and cosmetology. We'd room together, study together, go out on double dates.

But the only way that was going to happen was if I got through school with flying colors.

My phone buzzed again.

Quincy: *Don't jizz on my bed.*

He added a crying laughing emoji.

I snorted. We had pushed our beds together the first week and never moved them apart. Momma bought queen size sheets and put them over the two smaller mattresses to keep us out of the dreaded crack in the middle. I always figured Q got the best end of the deal because he liked to sprawl out. I kept to my own little area.

I sighed and absently ran a hand over his side of the bed.

I missed him.

I turned from my musings back to the movie. *Aladdin*. I loved all things Disney. Period. *Aladdin* struck something in me. Poor guy, coming from nothing, falling in love with the princess.

I wasn't in love with a princess. I wasn't *in love* with anyone.

Quincy: *You still jerkin' off? Thinking of me? Perv.*

I laughed again, but my dick was taking things a lot more seriously. I was sixteen years old. I think it was like a mandate or something that I had to jack off as many times as day as possible. I never went overboard. A couple times a day, especially in the shower, seemed completely reasonable. Q talked about jacking off incessantly. I immediately imagined him stroking himself and got harder.

What the hell?

I wouldn't think of my foster-turned-adopted brother while I jacked off.

Next to his bed.

I *couldn't* think of Quincy while I pumped my hard cock in my hand.

With his pillow so close and smelling like him.

I squinted my eyes closed and tried to think of anything sexy while I stroked myself. My tip was leaking, and I smeared it around. My balls drew up tight and I knew I was going to come. The last image in my head as I painted my stomach was of Quincy squeezing his thick, throbbing cock and exploding.

Shit.

Fuck.

What the actual hell?

I had never really found myself attracted to any girls at school. They were pretty and I wanted to style their hair and do their makeup, but I didn't think about their boobs or their butts.

I found the guys at school somewhat more appealing. But I always found my head categorizing them as taller than Quincy, shorter than Quincy, or eyes not as great as Quincy's. The comparisons went on forever.

With a tissue, I wiped the spunk from my stomach as these realizations hit me. It wasn't that I'd never considered these things. It was just that I'd never allowed myself to think about what they meant.

Okay, so I was a normal, hormonal, horny, and curious teen guy. Nothing wrong with that. I'd been texting with Q before my solo session, that was probably why he popped into my mind.

And all the times I'd subconsciously compared other guys to Quincy? He was my best friend, my brother, and I spent almost all of my time with him. He was what I knew. It was normal to compare.

Right?

I wasn't sure why, but I was having a lot harder time wrapping my brain around what it meant that I'd just jacked off to an image of Quincy than the fact that I found guys more attractive than girls.

Shit.

I couldn't like Quincy.

He was my brother.

Okay, not my blood-related brother. But still.

Plus, there was *no way* in hell that Q felt that way about me. He talked about girls a lot. I didn't think he had a girlfriend, but he was always asking me if I thought certain girls were pretty.

No way he'd be picturing me while he jacked off.

I sighed. My head and heart were heavy with confusion.

I turned back to my movie and watched Aladdin pine after Jasmine.

* * *

QUINCY FLOPPED on the bed and scared the shit out of me. "Dude, let's do something."

He got back from Max's house early that morning and was clearly itching for something to do. Momma and Pops had taken their two current foster kids for family visits and wouldn't be back until the next day.

"You could do your homework," I suggested as I read my book assigned for next week's classwork.

"Yuck, no." Q bounced on the bed. "We could watch porn."

I snorted. "Momma would skin us alive."

"Nah, she won't know. We'll use the old laptop we use for movies." He elbowed me. "Come on."

I shrugged. "Whatever." I knew the basics of sex and nothing about watching a guy screw some woman on a screen seemed like entertainment to me. But I had a hard time telling Quincy no.

"How about we drink some of Pops' moonshine?"

"You trying to get us killed?"

"Just want to do something different. Don't plan on getting drunk, just want to taste it and want my best friend to do it with me."

I rolled my eyes. "Fine. But I don't want to be drunk tonight or sick tomorrow."

"No worries. We'll do three shots and that's all. Pour it and put it away before we even take the drinks so we're not tempted to get it out again." Quincy bounded from the bed and headed out the door. "Come on, G, let's be wild."

Knowing I'd actually rather stay in bed and read, I

closed the book with a sigh and followed him out the door.

Quincy led me to the basement of the house and made me hold a dusty old flashlight as he sorted through cobweb covered bottles until he found what he was looking for. He pulled it out and held it up, triumphant in his discovery.

"How do you even know that's alcohol?" I wrinkled my nose.

Q pointed to the worn old label. Much of the writing was worn off, but I could see the word moonshine and the number 100 proof. I had no clue what that meant, but I accepted that the bottle was indeed at least alcohol.

"Hand me those cups." Quincy gestured to the six little Dixie cups he'd had me bring to the basement. "We'll pour it down here and then get our asses back upstairs. Less temptation." He shivered. "Plus, this basement freaks me the fuck out."

I laughed as I sat the six little cups on the dusty table. "Yeah, it's creepy down here."

"When I was little, I swore this house, or at least the basement, was haunted." Quincy laughed as he poured about an inch of liquid into each of the cups before putting on the lid and slipping the bottle back to its original spot. "Okay, let's go."

We tramped up the steps and locked the basement door behind us.

By the time we were back on our bed, I didn't care a

bit about the moonshine or the porn, but I was enjoying every second of having Q back home.

Quincy took a whiff of the alcohol and shuddered. "God, that smells terrible."

I followed suit and figured I'd likely gag trying to swallow it.

"Okay, three shots, ready?" Quincy held up one cup.

I grimaced and nodded.

We quickly drank the first and then second cups. The liquid burned badly, and I felt it go all the way down to catch fire in my stomach. For a couple seconds, I couldn't even breathe. My guts roiled in threat of upchucking.

Quincy let out a roar. "Ahhhh, it burns! Come on, last one!"

"I can't." I shook my head and wiped tears from my eyes.

"Just one more!"

"No, you can do yours. But I'll puke if I drink another."

Quincy shrugged. "Okay, okay. I'll probably puke too. Let's be done."

We crossed the hall to the bathroom and poured out the third shots before stacking the empty cups and wrapping them in toilet paper and shoving them to the bottom of the trashcan.

By the time we walked back into the bedroom, we notice that the effects of the moonshine were starting.

"My head feels funny." I blinked a few times to clear my vision.

"Your words sound funny," Quincy commented as he flopped down on the bed. "My face feels hot. Is your face hot?"

I burped and giggled. "My face feels weird, not hot."

"Time for porn!" Quincy rolled over and pulled the laptop from the floor. "I hear guys on the team talking about sites all the time." He typed in an address and waited for the site to load. "We'll have to try different ones because you can only watch clips without a subscription."

I snorted. "I'm sure Momma would be fine with us signing up if we told her it was educational." I couldn't stop laughing.

Quincy joined in. "Veeerrrry educational."

"Are we drunk? Is this what drunk feels like? It's not too bad." My teeth were sort of tingly and everything was funny, but I didn't feel too bad.

"I think this is buzzed," Quincy corrected. "I don't mind this feeling."

"Yeah, but if I have to drink moonshine to get this feeling, I'll likely never feel it again."

"Truth." Quincy grimaced. "Can you still feel it in your throat?"

I nodded. "It's so bad."

Q clicked a video clip, and we quickly shut up. By the time we'd reached the end of the various two-minute promo clips, I was hard and assumed he was too. In my slightly inebriated state, I was able to admit to myself that the men in the videos were a lot more appealing than the women.

Quincy adjusted himself quickly before clicking on another link. "Let's see what this one is."

And we found ourselves watching two men. Kissing. Touching. Having sex. With each other.

Everything the other videos had been missing, met me right on the screen with the gay couple.

"Holy hell," Quincy whispered. "Did you know this kind of porn existed?"

"I haven't spent a lot of time thinking about types of porn." I was glad the room was somewhat dark so I could palm my hard-on without calling much attention to myself.

"Do you like this?"

I shrugged in the dim darkness not wanting to give myself away with an answer.

"It's different than the guy girl stuff. Like not bad or better, just different. The girls were pretty and stuff, but the guys seem..." he trailed off.

"More," I choked out. "They seem more. More powerful, more equal, more—I don't even know how to describe it—but yeah, it's different." My head swam. Whether from the alcohol or the hormones or the lack of blood because it was all in my dick, I didn't know.

"Look how they touch each other." Quincy let out a whoosh of air. "Just jackin' each other off."

"Mmhm," I mumbled, trying to think of some way to answer that wouldn't expose how fucking turned on I was.

Quincy pushed the laptop to the foot of the bed.

"We should do that." He turned to me with a goofy grin and glassy eyes.

"You're drunk." I pushed him and laughed when all I really wanted to do was shuck my pants and let him grab my dick.

"No, I'm slightly buzzed. Big difference." Quincy glanced at my crotch. "Come on. We're both turned on, so let's see what those guys liked so much."

I rolled my eyes. "They like it because they are getting paid to get naked and bone whoever happens to be on the set. Porn isn't real life."

Quincy shook his head. "No, they might be getting paid, and I'm sure porn isn't super realistic. But there's no doubt they liked what they were doing to each other."

I stared at him. I wanted to feel his hand on me. I wanted to feel his hard cock in my fist. "Would you be wanting to do this if we weren't buzzed?"

"I always want to try something new, and I always want to be with you." Quincy shrugged. "Maybe the moonshine got me brave enough to try it." He paused. "Wait, do you want to? I won't force you to do anything. Never. I know I talk you into a lot of stuff, but this shit is different. Your body, your rules and all that. If you don't want my hand on you, just say the word."

My heart clenched. That was my Quincy, always looking out for me. "I'll try it."

"Say the full words. I gotta know you're totally on board."

"You can jack me off." My face flushed hot. "What about you? Are you sure this isn't just the alcohol?"

Quincy held up two fingers. "Scouts honor. You can jack me off."

I snorted. "You were never a Scout."

Quincy laughed and shimmied his shorts and boxer briefs down his legs. "Come on. Let's do this."

I lifted my hips and pushed down my shorts.

Q and I sat with our backs propped up on pillows at the head of the bed. We glanced at each other's hard-ons and a fire could have been lit with the heat that filled my cheeks. I'd seen other dicks before. Gym class was a lesson in various body parts. But Quincy's cock mesmerized me.

"Touch yourself," Quincy demanded.

Without a second thought, I took myself in my hand and stroked slowly. Quincy mirrored the action. We both looked to the porn scene frozen on the screen at the foot of the bed. Q groaned a little and slid his gaze my way.

"Can I do yours?" His words were quiet and breathy.

I nodded and moved my hand.

Quincy slowly took me in his hand, hesitantly, watching my face the whole time. "This okay?"

I nodded again and watched as his strong hand fisted around my hard length and began to stroke. His hand felt amazing.

"You can touch me if you want." Quincy had his right hand on me as he continued to stroke himself with his left.

When I reached to take his cock in my left hand, Q moved his hand away and let me grip his throbbing cock.

"This okay?" I asked as I pumped him soft and slow.

Quincy grunted. "You can be rougher."

"You too," I suggested.

We fell into a rhythm of pumping fists, rocking hips, and panting breaths.

"I want to watch you come. Do it on my hand," Quincy commanded. "Are you close?"

I nodded.

"Squeeze me tighter, I'm about to explode."

Three more strokes of my fist and Quincy shot his load all over my hand. The sight of his jizz dripping over my fingers went straight to my balls, and my cock jerked as I spilled into Q's hand.

"Probably better clean up." I slowly let loose of his softening dick. I grabbed a towel from the clothes basket and wiped my hand before wiping my shaft.

"Shit, better do a load of laundry. We both have spunk all over our shirts."

I winced when I saw the cum stains on my shirt and his. "Yeah, sounds good."

Quincy bounded from bed. "Throw me that towel and your shirt. I'll start a load. You can shower up here, and I'll grab the one downstairs."

So, we weren't going to speak of what we'd just done. Okay.

I tossed him the dirty towel and shirt before grabbing a fresh towel and heading to the bathroom. I heard the water in the laundry room start before the shower downstairs was turned on.

By the time I returned to the bedroom, Quincy had tucked himself under his blankets and rolled to his side, his back facing my side of the bed.

I drew in a deep breath.

Did he regret what we'd done?

Did I regret it? No. I had enjoyed what we'd done. But I hoped like hell it hadn't ruined anything between us.

I didn't really want to think about what had just happened in regards to me and another guy. But it had been great with Quincy.

However, the way he shut down afterward proved that he definitely didn't feel about me the same way I felt about him.

THE NEXT MORNING, I woke when Q rolled from bed. He padded across the floor and out the door. A few moments later, I heard the dryer start. When he returned, Quincy dressed quickly and left the room again.

I got up, dressed, and followed him down the stairs.

I found him in the kitchen.

"Hey, you okay?" I started the kettle for hot water.

Quincy popped a pod into the coffee machine. "Yeah, I'm fine."

"You wish we hadn't done that?" I leaned against the counter and crossed my arms.

Quincy hung his head. "I don't know. It felt great, right?"

I nodded.

"I guess I'm just freakin' out that it will mess something up between us. I liked it, and I don't regret it, but I don't want it to push us apart."

"Nothing can push us apart, Q."

"Can we chalk it up to friends getting horny and experimenting? Leave it at that?" Quincy's eyes begged as he asked his question.

"Sure, Q." I wanted to hug him, wanted to hear him say that what we did meant more to him. But I just fixed my tea and we went about our day as normal as possible.

A week later, Quincy was gone.

3

QUINCY

MY DAD WAS NOW BACK in the states for at least two years and wanted me to live with him. It meant leaving Momma, Pops, and Griffin, but I couldn't turn it down. I was sixteen and had spent most of my life away from my dad. He was a good man, and I wanted to live with him. I lost my mom before I was even an hour old and it hurt not knowing her. My dad had taken care of me and spent as much time with me as he could, but working overseas had made that hard. Knowing he had a solid two years in the states meant we could have a good chunk of time together.

So, a week after Griffin and I lost our minds and jacked each other off, I moved to the other side of the country for Dad's job. I missed my best friend like crazy. I also missed Momma and Pops, but I missed Griffin even more. I missed his damn dancing and makeup. I missed him crying at Disney movies. I missed sleeping next to him every night.

We kept in touch by text and the occasional phone or video call over those two years. But I had a lot going on, especially with sports, at my new school. I planned to go to college on a football scholarship, but I played any and every sport available. And Grif was working his ass off to graduate. He had a part time job along with extracurriculars, volunteerism, and school work. He was determined to go to college and get as many scholarships as possible.

The two years I was away from Griffin taught me a lot about myself. I wasn't great at school, but I got by. I loved all things sports and excelled at football; my plans for college still involved a sports management degree. And I definitely gravitated toward guys in the attraction department. That wasn't a new development; I had been finding myself more and more attracted to males than females since before Grif and I messed around. Finding ourselves on that gay porn site had not been an accident on my part.

I kissed a few guys and messed around a bit after leaving Momma and Pops', but none of them felt right. It wasn't like I should be kissing and messing around with a girl; I definitely found the guys attractive. The problem was that anything I did with guys always made me think of Griffin. I wanted to go back to that night in our room. I wanted to kiss him, taste him, and tell him it all meant more than just messing around. But did Griffin see me as more than a best friend and brother?

"You ready for graduation?" I asked one night while we video chatted. I was supposed to be doing homework, but I had taken a break to play video games. Dad was in his downstairs office. We'd had our usual dinner together before he went back to his work. If we weren't at one of my games, Dad and I always made sure to spend some time together on evenings and weekends.

Griffin was actually doing homework because that's what he did, what he was good at. He groaned. "So ready. This is my last big project and then I should be done." He had books spread out on the bed—our bed, a pencil in hand and one behind his ear.

"What are you working on?"

"It's a final project for my business math class. If I can get a good grade, I can skip the lower level one in college and go straight into the higher class."

"You got it. You've always been good at all the school stuff."

"Thanks. It's been fun because the project has me thinking about all the shit I want to do with my own business. You know, the hair and makeup and all of that."

Griffin had known he would go into cosmetology school whether or not he went to college since we first started talking about college. But if it all worked out the way he now planned, he'd be doing cosmetology school along with a business degree.

"Everything coming through the way you need it to as far as college and aid and scholarships?" I hated that

Griffin had to worry so much about getting into college when my dad easily paid for anything my football scholarship didn't cover.

"Yes, it all seems to be working out." Griffin bit his lip while he spoke, most of his attention on his homework.

"Just like we planned." I finished the world before pausing my game. "You been going out with anyone?" Subtlety wasn't my strong suit.

Griffin dropped his pencil and looked directly at the screen. "Huh?"

"You work all the time. Homework, school, part time job, helping Momma and Pops. You need to go out and have fun."

"I don't really have a lot of time."

"That's the point."

"I've gone out with a few groups from school. Coffee once. A movie. One time we all went to a party but it was completely lame. I called Pops to come get me. Parties are not my scene."

"You dating anyone?"

Griffin scoffed. "No, not a lot of time for romance, ya know? I thought about trying to be more adventurous this summer, but I'm going to be working full time trying to save up money for school. So, I think I'll just continue being the scrawny introvert who enjoys a good book, a great palette of eyeshadow, and a moving Disney movie."

"I think I'm gay," I blurted.

Griffin stared at the screen for so long I feared our connection had frozen.

"Grif?"

"I'm here. I'm just…" Griffin mumbled. "You think you're gay?"

"Okay, I know I'm gay. I just wasn't sure how to bring it up. I don't want you to think differently about me."

Griffin laughed. "No worries, promise."

"Yeah?"

"Yeah, because I'm gay too. I've known for a while. Just wasn't sure how to bring it up either." Griffin stared at me.

I swallowed hard. I wasn't surprised that Griffin was gay, I guess I'd always sort of known. Was it the right time to tell G that I wanted more with him? Would he be on the same page?

"But I promise, Q, us being gay will do *nothing* to our friendship. I swear. We can stay best friends and brothers. I won't let this interfere in what we have. Like, I'm not even dating or messing around. I barely even know any other gay guys around here. But you and I are good, always." Griffin's gaze bore into the screen. "What we have is so important to me. I can't lose my brother and best friend. We'll be fine, right?"

And there it was. Griffin wasn't attracted to me. He just wanted to stay best friends and brothers. I was helpless to go against anything Griffin wanted. So, I nodded. "Definitely. Nothing between us will change. But any guy you date has to pass my inspection." My gut twisted with those words. The thought of Griffin with anyone but me was torture.

Griffin winced a bit and laughed. "Same for you. Don't think we'll get to college and you can just prance guys in and out without my approval."

We ended the video chat with the promise to talk soon.

But the rest of the school year and summer was so busy that Griffin and I managed to only text. We texted daily, which was nice, but it wasn't the same. I missed seeing him. But maybe it was for the best. I needed to remember that Griffin was my family, he wasn't a love interest. No matter how badly my heart and body wanted him to be.

I spent the summer of my eighteenth year trying to forget how much I wanted to be with my best friend. I made out with every willing guy I could get my hands on. I had a lot of fun, but those moments brought me no real satisfaction. I had a feeling that the only way I would ever quench the thirst in my blood was with Griffin. And that wasn't what he wanted, so I had to respect that and move on.

* * *

ONE WEEK before I moved to college, I was on a second official date with Jaylin. He was a nice guy, went to my school, and was fun to spend time with. Jaylin and I had hung out in groups of friends all school year before he finally asked me out. The first date had gone well, and I agreed to a second easily.

We sat in a coffee shop drinking lattes and listening to a girl play acoustic guitar on a tiny stage. Jaylin sat close, his thigh touching mine. The closeness wasn't uncomfortable, it just wasn't keeping my interest. My thoughts were on Griffin.

I had an unreasonable fear I'd get to college and Griffin wouldn't show up.

Scholarships would fall through.

He'd change his mind.

Something.

There was no guarantee we'd end up rooming together. We'd both put down the other's name on our room requests, but nothing was set in stone. I hadn't gotten any roommate information yet, and I assumed Grif hadn't either. Unless he just wasn't telling me about it.

"So, heading to college next week?" Jaylin's words pulled me from my thoughts.

I nodded and sipped my drink. "Yeah, got a lot to do between now and then."

Jaylin moved even closer and nuzzled my neck. "Gonna miss having you around. You want to get out of here?"

I downed the rest of my latte and scooted from the booth. "Sure, let's go."

Jaylin drove back to his house so I could get my car.

"You want to come in? My parents are out."

I shrugged. I knew I wasn't being fair to Jaylin, but I was preoccupied with college and Griffin.

We stopped in the kitchen.

"You want something to drink?"

"Nah, I'm good." I leaned against the counter.

Jaylin crossed the room to stand in front of me. He was close enough I could feel his heat, breathe in his scent. He was an attractive guy. Jaylin stepped closer and gripped my hips. His mouth took mine in a soft, easy kiss as his hard length nudged my inner thigh.

My mind flashed to an image of Griffin's cock in my hand, spilling over my fingers as he came. I wanted Grif's cock rocking into me. I wanted Grif's lips on mine. I wanted Grif in my arms. I sighed.

"Wow, you're so not into this, huh?" Jaylin smirked as he ended the kiss and took a step back. "Who is it?"

I started to protest, but realized there was no need. "Guy from home. I miss him. He'll be at college with me and that's on my mind a lot."

"Something happen that you could start back up?"

"Nah, I mean, something happened, but we were just kids."

"You gonna at least ask him out?" Jaylin raised a brow.

Griffin's gorgeous face flashed in my mind along with his words, *What we have is so important to me. I can't lose my brother and best friend. We'll be fine, right?*

"He doesn't feel that way about me. We're just friends." I shrugged and checked the time.

"Some of the best relationships start as just friends."

"Some of the best friendships are ruined by trying to be anything else." I pulled my keys from my pocket. "Sorry for being distant and no fun tonight. Let's keep in touch, yeah?" I pulled Jaylin into a hug.

He gave me a smile and a wave as I left his house.

How in the hell was I going to find something with a guy if every time I tried, I was struck with thoughts and images of Griffin-freakin-Murphy-Sanders. And it wasn't like I could even explain it to anyone. Yeah, I'm hot for my best friend who also happens to be my adopted brother who I've known since I was ten. But he doesn't see me like that so I have to secretly pine away for him while trying to relieve an itch with other guys who can't even hold a candle to Griffin. And all my heart and body want is something with someone I can't have.

Shit.

I ran a hand over my face as I started my car and headed home.

Starting college and having Griffin nearby was what I'd been looking so forward to for such a long time, but I was beginning to think it could be a tortuous experience if my heart and dick couldn't get themselves under control.

4

GRIFFIN

THE DAY MOMMA and Pops moved me into college was as surreal as they come. Except for the day I found out I was going to get to stay with Momma and Pops forever, moving into college was the most amazing dream-come-true I'd ever experienced.

"You excited to see Quincy?" Momma asked from the front seat.

"Yeah. Can't wait to get moved in and spend some time settling in and exploring campus before classes start." I sat in the middle section of the van surrounded by my luggage and dorm room supplies. Excited to see Quincy was an understatement. I'd missed my brother so much my chest sometimes ached with wishing he was back home. But excited wasn't the only feeling rushing through my veins. Anxiety, trepidation, wanting, and unsureness warred with each other as I thought about seeing Quincy again.

"Sure wish the college would have let us know if you guys get to room together." Momma pointed toward a parking spot, and Pops maneuvered the van into it.

"I guess we're lucky to know we are at least in the same building." I'd recently gotten a letter stating I'd be in Green Hall, and Quincy had texted to tell me he was also in Green.

"I'm glad you both decided to take advantage of the early move-in date. Hopefully it will be less crowded." Momma exited the van. "Duane, you stay with the van. I'll take Griffin in and get his room assignment. If there's a line, I'll send him out with a cart if there's one available so you can start loading the luggage."

Pops gave a quiet nod. He never had too much to say, but he was an amazing man and loved Momma beyond measure. Pops had been a quiet strength from the very first day I walked into the Sanders home, and I hoped that someday I'd be half the man he was.

When Momma and I entered Green Hall, we were met with a welcome blast of cool air and a fairly short check-in line.

"Griffin, grab that cart and take it to Pops. Don't dawdle, this line looks to be moving pretty quickly." Momma hefted her purse onto her shoulder and shuffled the folder and papers she had brought with her. She had some experience with settling her son, Max, into college, but she was definitely exuding momma bear vibes getting me moved in. Momma had been a rock for me throughout school and scholarship applications.

I rolled out the cart to Pops. He met me with a smile and a pat on the back. "Proud of you, just like I was for Max and I am for Quincy. Good to see all my sons being so great."

I clenched my jaw and fought back the stinging tears. "Thanks, Pops. Love you." I gave him a quick hug.

"Better get back in there before Marlene has both our hides."

Momma was next in line when I returned.

"Here, you can take care of checking in." Momma handed me the papers and folder.

"Welcome to Green Hall." The smiley girl behind the table greeted me when it was my turn. "Name?"

"Griffin Murphy-Sanders." I always got a surge of pride stating my full name. It was in memory of my mom, proof I'd overcome a shitty past, and assurance that I had a forever family to love and support me.

The girl scanned the list. "Ah, here you are. Room 1012. Here are the keys, dorm rules, your Resident Assistant's information, and a map of the building and campus. The elevators are down the hall, mailboxes are next to the elevators. If you've got questions or need help, look for someone in a green shirt. We all live in Green Hall and are happy to help." She gave me a smile and a wink.

Momma tsked as we walked away. "Poor girl. Shouldn't even waste her time."

I snorted. Momma and I had never really talked about my sexuality, but I knew that she knew I was gay and was completely fine with it. She also knew Quincy was gay. I adored Momma and Pops, and Max, for not making anything difficult for Quincy and me.

"Let's get started on hauling up your stuff." Momma bustled toward the van. Pops had the cart full and secure, just waiting for Momma to give the word. "I can carry these two bags. Grif, you take your backpack and that tote. We'll get the rest after we go for last minute supplies, groceries, and lunch."

We only had to wait for a couple minutes for an open elevator. We got off the elevator and turned to the left, a right, and then a left. Room 1012 was the last room in the hall.

My hand shook as I unlocked the door and my breath caught when I pushed the door open. As a kid who spent his first ten years in run down apartments, roach infested hotel rooms, and the backseat of a car when my mom couldn't gather enough cash to pay rent, this college dorm room seemed like a mansion.

Momma and Pops house was big and comfy and provided for all of my needs. But it was *their* house.

This room, this *suite*, was mine. Sure, I'd have to share it with someone. God willing I'd be sharing it with Quincy. Only time would tell. But the room was mine. The kitchen was mine. The bathroom was mine. My eyes stung with tears I hadn't expected.

The suite door opened into the living room which was attached to a small kitchen and breakfast nook on the right. To the left were two bedrooms which shared an adjoining bathroom. The colors of all the rooms were neutral beiges, tans, creams, and browns. Each bedroom and the living room had a tasteful, small ceiling light. Two floor lamps adorned the living room between a plain but functional couch and two recliners. The kitchen was open and airy with bright track lighting. The bathroom had a medicine cabinet behind the mirrored doors and soft white bulbs above the sink. Each bedroom had a desk and lamp, a dresser, a twin bed, and a small closet.

"Well, this is just as cute as can be. Let's get it cleaned spic-n-span before we unpack." Momma opened the tote of cleaning supplies she'd brought. "Pops, you start in the bathroom. Use this spray and cloth. Toilet, sink, shower and bath." She handed Pops the cleaner and rag. "Griffin, you vacuum while I spray your mattress with disinfectant. I'll spray the other mattress too. Even if Quincy isn't your roommate, no one deserves a dirty mattress. We'll let them sit with the spray while we're gone. Lord knows the germs on those things. After the mattresses, I'll move to the kitchen. You can meet me there. We'll make sure the refrigerator is spotless before we fill it. I'm guessing that dishwasher hasn't been cleaned very well. I brought a disinfecting pod, we'll run it through while we work." Momma gave commands like a drill sergeant, and Pops and I set to work.

In less than forty-five minutes, we had the whole suite spotless.

"It already feels better in here. A good cleaning is the best way to make a place feel like yours. I pray it's good luck that I cleaned the second room just as well as yours; maybe it will bring Quincy as your roommate." Momma winked.

My phone buzzed and I answered Quincy's call. "Speak of the devil. What's up, Q?"

"Man, Dad and I are getting off the elevator. What room did you get?"

"Room 1012," I answered as the door burst open.

"No fucking way!" Quincy dropped his bags, crossed the room in three strides and yanked me into a hug as Momma scolded him for his language, but she held a hand to her mouth to cover a watery smile.

I let Q bounce and jostle and squeeze me as we both laughed.

"We did it, Grif! I don't know how, but we did it."

I smiled. "Maybe believing in something long enough made it happen."

Max coughed. "Or your Momma made *several* calls to the housing department."

"You made just as many." Momma crossed her arms and leveled a look at her son.

"Fine, we both made calls." Max shrugged.

"That Sarah is such a sweetie. I knew she'd do her best to make it happen." Momma put her arms around Quincy and me and held us close. "I wasn't sure how I'd deal with my boys being gone if they weren't together."

Quincy took time to hug Momma and Pops while I let Max pull me into a hug.

"I think lunch is in order. We've already cleaned the whole suite. Let's go eat." Momma picked up her purse. "Max, can you stay?"

"I can swing lunch, but I have to head out after that." Quincy's dad had moved for his job and was closer to Momma and Pops again.

"We'll take the boys shopping for any supplies and groceries they didn't pack." Momma marched to the door. "Boys, where do you want to eat?"

"Let's do somewhere nice, not fast food." Quincy nudged me. "I'm sure Grif and I will get tired of fast food. What about that steak place I saw a few blocks from here?"

"Steak sounds perfect," Pops interjected.

We pushed the cart into the hall.

"If you're done with that, can we borrow it?" A girl with red hair asked with a smile.

"Sure thing, saves us a trip to return it." I let the girl pull the cart from my grasp.

The five of us piled into the elevator.

"I can't believe you guys knew we were going to be roommates and kept it a secret." I shook my head.

"We didn't *know*," Max stated. "We had high hopes, but the housing department wouldn't give any guarantees."

"I think I'll bake some cookies for Sarah. Such a nice girl." Momma hefted her purse and watched the numbers fall from ten to the ground floor.

"Max, you drive yourself so you can leave when you need to. Boys, you ride with us."

Quincy put me in a headlock and ruffled my hair. "I just can't believe it all worked out. God, I've missed you, G."

We arrived at the restaurant not long after and lucked out by getting a table right away.

"See, another good reason for moving in early. Places will be *packed* when the majority of the students move in." Momma nodded as she perused the menu.

We spent the next hour laughing, eating, and enjoying the company.

Despite Momma's protests, Max grabbed the bill. Once outside, Max gave hugs and goodbyes and we watched him drive away.

"How long will he be gone?" I glanced at Q.

"He's in the states for a while still even with the recent move. Maybe until this time next year. So, I'll see him, no worries." Quincy opened the door for Momma.

The next hour and a half was spent filling a cart to the brim with cleaning supplies, kitchen and bathroom necessities, bedding, food, and a few décor pieces that Momma deemed necessary.

"This will be a good baseline for you boys. You can pick up other things as needed." Momma scanned her list one last time as we headed to get in line.

I was immediately reminded of the shopping trip Momma, Quincy, and I had gone on when I first moved in with them. My heart filled with love and appreciation.

"And we're only two hours away. We'll visit and bring supplies when we can." Momma was still talking as she loaded the groceries onto the check-out belt.

Quincy and I headed to the bagging area and helped load the bags back into the cart.

When we got back to the dorm, Momma set to work stocking the kitchen.

"Duane, you help the boys get their beds made up. I would prefer to wash the sheets first, but there's no way around it for now. You boys promise me you'll wash them at least once a week."

Pops tossed bedding sets at Quincy and me. "Let's go."

As we went to work on Quincy's bed first, Pops took a look at the internet access ports. "Looks like the Wifi should be easy to set up. Probably want to make sure you've got your phones and computers set up and working with no problems *before* you break out the moonshine and porn sites. Wouldn't want the campus tech guys to stumble across that. 'Course, I'm guessing they've seen it all." Pops didn't even turn to look at us as he pondered over the technology outlets.

Quincy and I stared at each other wide-eyed.

"You knew?" Quincy squeaked.

"Boy, you're lucky I ran across those porn sites instead of Momma. You'd both be dead with no hope of college."

"How'd you know about the moonshine?" I put Quincy's pillow into the case.

We walked through the bathroom to my room and started the bed-making process again.

"I gathered the trash. Smelled like a distillery in your bathroom trash can. I dug deeper and found the evidence of your little party." Duane chuckled. "Oh boy, Momma would have killed you a second time if she'd found that."

Quincy and I laughed awkwardly.

Did Pops know what Quincy and I had *done* to each other along with the porn and moonshine? Oh my God.

"Duane, you almost done? We better head home. We need to pick up the little ones." Momma hollered from the kitchen.

Hugs and words of love and thanks were exchanged before we wished Momma and Pops safe travels and sent them on their way.

Quincy and I flopped onto the couch.

"Can you believe it? It's like we're sitting here watching our dream play out in front of us. This place is ours. We live together. Everything we planned is happening."

Quincy spoke the words and my heart felt every bit of them.

"Yeah, it's sort of surreal. I keep thinking it's a dream. I'll be heartbroken if I wake up."

Quincy hummed. "Man, what do you want to do?" Quincy rolled his head to look at me. "Go out? Find a party? Stay in?"

I grimaced.

"Stay in, that's my Grif." Quincy slapped my leg.

"You don't have to entertain me," I started. "I can kick back with a movie and pizza and hit the sack early. Maybe we explore the campus tomorrow?"

Quincy frowned. "Do you not *want* to spend time with me? I thought at least tonight would be just us."

My heart fluttered. Quincy wanted to spend his night with me.

"I'd love to hang with you. I've missed having you around. But I know your idea of fun doesn't usually match mine. If you want a party, I'm fine staying here."

"No way. Pizza and movie night at home. It's a plan." Quincy gave me a big goofy smile.

My heart stopped. How was I going to live with Quincy and not continue falling head over heels in love with him? It started eight years ago and being apart for two years hadn't eased the ache. But we were friends. Period.

Thirty minutes later, we had a large pizza, two sodas, a bag of chips, and two king size candy bars spread out on the tiny coffee table.

"What are we watching?" Quincy fiddled with the television and game system he'd brought with him. Clearly presents from Max.

"We could binge a few episodes of something rather than a movie." I wasn't sure how well I'd be able to focus on anything.

"What about the new season of Queer Eye?"

"Yaaaas, Queen!" I laughed. "Seriously, I love that show. But you know I'll cry."

"No worries. I'll dry your tears."

Quincy hit play and we tore into the food.

Three episodes later, my napkin was a soggy mess, and I couldn't stop sniffling.

Quincy chuckled and put his arm around me. "Grif, it's a happy show."

I nodded. "I know. It's just so inspirational. They take these people who have lost sight of how beautiful and special they are and give them the tools and skills to let their gorgeous souls shine through. There's nothing better than watching a person learn to love themselves."

"Yeah, it's a great show. They do amazing things. I hope I can be that for someone someday."

I scrunched up my face. "Someday? You do realize that you did this for me, right?"

Q laughed. "Hardly."

"No, for real. Ten-year-old Quincy totally Queer-Eyed me. Style? Check. Remember when you helped me pick out clothes and shoes? Culture? Check. You always encouraged me to talk about my mom and the good memories. Grooming? Check. I'd still be having Momma cut my nails if you didn't force me to learn how to do it myself."

Quincy snorted. "You were scared to death to do your own nail clipping. I don't know how you thought those little clippers were going to cut off your whole finger."

I ignored him and continued my train of thought. "Food and wine? Check. You taught me how to make my own peanut butter and jelly sandwich. *And* you showed me that moonshine is basically like drinking turpentine. Renovation? Check. The night you helped me slide my bed across your bedroom and snug it up against yours was the start of a friendship that may never make sense, but it's my heart and soul."

Quincy's face was serious. "Okay, I can see it. I'd do it all over again because you've given me just as much. Watching you grow from that scared, traumatized, lonely little kid into a unique, intelligent, successful man was as good for my heart as it was for you." He paused. "But what do you mean that our friendship doesn't make sense?"

It was my turn to snort. "Seriously?"

Quincy nodded and waited for me to speak.

I turned toward him and pulled a leg under me. "Look at us. I'm this pasty, scrawny, fem guy; you're this glowing, muscular, tough guy. I love makeup and dance, I cry over sappy movies, I love to have my nails painted; you love working out, action and adventure movies, and you excel at anything to do with sports. Not to mention I came from a traumatic background filled with neglect, drugs, and a homicide/suicide; you have a solid family and money for anything you may need." I shrugged. "We have nothing in common. We never should have ended up as friends."

"Do you regret it?"

"Never!" I laid a hand on his leg. "I'm grateful beyond words every day that I landed in your home and Momma stuck us together. I'm just saying, if circumstances were different, we likely would have never become friends. We're too different. I never would have fit into your life without Momma making it happen."

"So, I'm so shallow that I never could have befriended you if Momma hadn't *made* me?" Quincy's tone held hurt.

I ran a hand over my face. "No, stop twisting what I'm saying."

He held my hand. "Different isn't bad. Friends don't have to be exactly the same. I love your makeup; you've got mad skills. I love your flashy nails, your dancing, and your tears over sappy movies. And stop saying *I* have a solid family; they're *your* family too. And we've got the papers to prove it."

I heard his words, but my focus was on our hands. I longed for Quincy to feel for me what I felt for him. My brain flashed images of us eating pizza, watching a movie, holding hands, kissing, and falling into bed. Together. Quincy's arms wrapped around me. Quincy loving me the same way I loved him. As my brother, as my best friend, *and* as my partner. My lover.

"Grif?" Quincy jostled my hand. "Where'd you go? Did you even hear a word I said?"

I smiled. "Yeah, I heard you. Look, we're as opposite as they get, but we work. Period. I'm blessed to have you as a brother and friend."

Quincy pressed his lips together in a slight smile. "Yeah. We *are* blessed. Brothers and friends. Couldn't ask for anything more, right?"

* * *

OVER THE NEXT WEEK, Quincy and I spent every day together. We explored the campus, looked into part-time job options, bought our books, went to the discount store to finalize our school supplies, and mapped out our classes.

I was scheduled for classes on Monday and Friday, plus two online classes along with my Tuesday, Wednesday, Thursday classes at the local cosmetology school.

Quincy had classes and practice every day.

We figured we'd have most of our evenings together and likely a lot of our weekends would match up.

"I'll have games, but you can come to those sometimes. And as soon as you're trained enough to handle this hotness," Quincy gestured up and down his body and ran his hands over his hair, "I'll allow you to cut my hair. But only once I deem you trustworthy." He laughed.

"Boy, you know I'm expert level, just need the license to prove it." I elbowed him.

The first week of classes hit us hard, but we soon settled into a routine.

Breakfast together. Tea for me, coffee for Quincy. We usually shared a box of cereal or toast. If one of us was feeling extra we might make eggs.

We had our own little suite, a routine, and we loved each other.

It was enough. It had to be enough. It should've been enough.

But it wasn't.

I wanted more.

I wanted so much more.

But I couldn't destroy a friendship by letting on that I loved Q as more than a brother and a friend.

So, I pushed down my feelings, played house with Quincy, threw myself into my classes, and pretended I wasn't in love with my best friend.

QUINCY

I WENT to my dad's over Fall Break. We had a nice visit. But I missed Griffin.

Me: *Don't miss me too much.*

Griffin: *I'll do my best.*

Me: *Whatcha doing?*

Griffin: *Watching a movie. Finished homework earlier.*

Me: *Lame. What else?*

Griffin: *Nothing else. Just watching this movie.*

Me: *Crying? Jacking off? Jacking off while you cry?*

Griffin: *I may have some tears. It's a heartwarming movie.*

Me: *Awwww, poor Grif. Jack off, it will make you feel better.*

Griffin: *Dude, if I jacked off as much as you insinuate I do, my dick would fall off.*

I snorted. I wanted to be on the couch, holding Grif as he cried. And jacking him off.

Fuck.

Me: *I'll be home tomorrow. We'll have the rest of the weekend to relax and just hang.*

Griffin: *Sounds good. See you then. Be safe driving.*

WHEN I GOT BACK to campus, Griffin and I spent the whole weekend with take-out, movies, and video games.

Sunday night we hit up a local coffee shop just to get out of the suite.

"Oh, look! A haunted house costume party." Grif took one of the flyers from a community bulletin board. "We should do this!"

"We should?"

Griffin shrugged. "You don't have to. It would just be fun to do costumes."

"You don't like parties or big groups of people." I crossed my arms and smirked.

"But I love makeup and costumes." Griffin's eyes lit up. "I'd probably only go if you went. The chance to show off makeup and costumes overrides my dislike of parties and big groups if you're there."

We spent the next couple weeks planning our costumes. Okay, *Griffin* spent the next couple weeks planning our costumes. I was on consult only. His idea for our costumes was perfect.

The day of the haunted house costume party was the absolute perfect fall day. Warm breeze and sunshine filtered through brightly colored leaves. The evening would be crisp and cool.

"We should give ourselves three hours to get ready." Griffin danced through the kitchen eating a piece of cold pizza.

"Three hours?" I gawked.

"From shower to final touches, yes. Three hours makes it so we're not rushed. I'll take care of my makeup first and then get yours started. We're walking to the party, right?"

I nodded and took a swig of soda.

"Okay, then we have a couple hours before we need to start the preparations."

"Nap?"

Griffin swallowed his pizza. "Movie?"

"Movies on a Saturday afternoon usually end in a nap."

"True."

We settled in to watch some random movie. Within moments, Griffin's head flopped back on the sofa and slid to the side until he collided with my shoulder.

I wanted to lay down and pull Griffin close.

I wanted my arms around him.

I wanted more.

But I let my head rest against his and closed my eyes.

I'd take what I could get.

"SHIT! WAKE UP!" Griffin startled awake next to me.

"We're thirty minutes past the scheduled preparation time." He jumped up and pulled me to my feet. "I'm going to shower and get started on my makeup. You can shower while I'm getting ready." With that, he rushed off.

The shower came on and I smiled. Seeing Griffin so pumped about something was great. And I loved that he was comfortable going to the party if I was with him. My heart swelled with a sense of pride that I'd be showing off his makeup skills with my costume. I wanted everyone to know he was my brother, and my best friend.

I paused.

I wanted everyone to know he was mine.

And he was, in a way. My best friend. My adopted brother.

But not mine in the way I most wanted.

When Griffin started singing Broadway tunes, I grinned from ear-to-ear. "Sing it, baby!" I hollered into the bathroom as I walked to my room to lay out my costume.

Grif had fashioned my costume from a very large, stretchy, green halter dress. He cut zig-zags along the bottom hem and made a belt from a darker green length of tulle. The green tights taunted me; they looked way to small, but Griffin promised they'd stretch to fit. The pink ballet-style house slippers were a nice touch. My wings were created from wire coat hangers and white pantyhose decorated with glitter paint. Griffin tried telling me about his plans for my hair and makeup, but

I knew it would be something I'd have to see to completely understand it.

By the time I was out of the shower, Griffin was well into his transformation. Dark green tunic top, light green leggings, brown slippers, and a green triangular felt hat with a feather. The outfit was quite simple. Griffin's hair was light and floppy, so he simply combed it forward and to the side. The makeup was anything but simple.

Griffin's eyes were beyond amazing. Bright green on the lid, a darker almost turquoise up to the brow bone, and a maroon liner on the top lid that winged out into a feather design. Glittery green liner sparkled on his lower lid, and long black lashes finished his look. The dark almost black forest green lipstick Griffin was applying made his perfect lips pop.

My dick wanted those lips to do nasty things.

Shit. I groaned.

"You like?" Griffin didn't take his eyes from the mirror.

"Amazing as usual."

"Get dressed. I want you in costume before I start on makeup and hair."

I pulled on the tights, adjusting my cock and hoping the tight material would help conceal my hard-on. The dress was easy enough to slip into. Never one to judge others for their likes or kinks, I ran my hands over the body skimming dress and definitely understood the appeal some men found in wearing more feminine clothes. "Wings now or later?" I stepped into the bathroom.

Griffin's breath caught. "Ohhh," he breathed out slowly. "That looks amazing. Oh, um, wings later. Yeah, wings later."

I chuckled. "Okay." I tossed the wings on my bed before pulling on the pink slippers.

"You ready?" Griffin asked from the bathroom. "I need extra time for your makeup, I'm better at doing my own."

"Yep, make me over, baby."

"I think the light is better in the kitchen. And I'll need you to sit."

We found ourselves in the kitchen, and I plopped into a chair as Griffin spread his supplies on the table.

Griffin frowned. "That puts you too low."

"Can you sit too?"

He pursed his lips. "I can try that." Griffin pulled a chair over to face mine and sat.

Our knees bumped and he groused. "I can't get close enough."

I grabbed his legs and hefted them over mine before pulling the chair closer. "Better?"

Griffin's cheeks pinked, but he nodded.

Forty-five minutes later, Griffin sighed. "There. Perfect. You want to see?"

"Of course."

He led me to the bathroom mirror, and I sucked in a breath.

"You like?"

"You're so damn talented, G. This is fabulous. I can't wait for everyone to see your skills. I'm like a walking advertisement for you."

Griffin had applied multiple small combs in my hair and attached long black hair to each comb. He pulled all the hair into a messy but expertly designed top knot adorned with sparkly green ribbons. My makeup was to die for, though. Light, glittery green outlined my entire eye area from corner to corner and bottom lid to brow bone. My top lid was swept with a darker green and a bright white liner with dramatic wings. Glittery white, green, and gold spots decorated my eyes from inner corner to temple on top and bottom. I pressed my lips together and smiled. Dark pink covered my lips.

"I love it. It's all so damn good."

Griffin smiled from ear-to-ear. "We are about ten minutes ahead of schedule. We should do pee breaks and final costume checks before we head out."

I nodded. "I need wing help."

"I'll be your wing man," Griffin joked.

Ten minutes later, we locked the suite and headed to the party.

We were instantly bombarded with compliments and people wanting pictures.

When we reached the sidewalk and had some time to ourselves, I glanced at Griffin. "Why Peter Pan and Tinkerbell?" I had been onboard since the first mention of the pair, but I hadn't thought to ask why.

Griffin smiled. "I don't know. I wanted a pair. Like salt and pepper or ketchup and mustard. But I wanted fun costumes and great makeup. Then I remembered a quote from *Peter Pan* and knew it was perfect."

I raised my brows and waited.

"In *Peter Pan* he says, 'You mean more to me than anyone in this whole world,' and that's how I feel about you."

The lump in my throat was hard to swallow and my eyes stung. "Damn it, don't make me cry. I'm not used to having makeup on; I don't want to mess it up." I sniffed. In my head, I vowed to watch *Peter Pan* soon.

The haunted house turned out to be superb. The hosts of the party had put a lot of work into the special effects. Griffin hated the jump-out-and-scare-you parts, but he was fascinated by all the great makeup on the haunted house participants.

The two of us definitely had the best makeup of all the party-goers. Griffin seemed to never tire of the compliments, and I'd never get tired of the proud feeling in my heart knowing I was with someone as amazing as him.

By the time we got home, I was beyond ready to shed the tights, and I was sure my mascara was running, but I'd loved every second of having Griffin by my side.

"I gotta piss," I announced as I unlocked the door. I rushed to the bathroom and relieved myself. "Hey, you want to play a game or watch a movie?" I asked after I'd finished and walked back into the dark living room. "Grif?" Shit. Had he already gone to bed? Damn. I thought we'd have a couple more hours together.

I tiptoed toward Griffin's door. Pressing my ear to it, I listened for a moment.

"Boo!" Griffin grabbed me from behind.

I would have pissed myself if I hadn't just used the restroom. I spun around, my heart in my chest, and lunged at Griffin. "Fuck, Grif! You almost gave me a heart attack."

Griffin couldn't stop laughing. "I was hiding on the other side of the couch. Oh my God, you jumped so much."

I picked him up and carried him toward the couch. "Not cool!"

Griffin's legs wrapped around me, and he wriggled in my arms. His movements threw me off balance and when my leg bumped into the arm of the couch, we both went down. Griffin landed with a 'oof' and I found myself between his legs.

"Shit, sorry. You okay?" I tried to ignore the fact that the only thing separating my cock from Grif's was some thin hosiery.

"Yeah, I'm good." Grif's laughter had dimmed and his decorated eyes widened as he stared up at me.

My chest heaved and my heart pounded.

Griffin's arms and legs wrapped around me.

I held him close. It was like a dream come true.

But, no. It couldn't be. I couldn't act on it. I wouldn't lose him.

I began to push up on my arms.

Griffin tightened his hold and pulled my face closer. His lips were on mine before I knew what was happening. I savored the sweet flavor of him as our mouths tested, tasted, and teased. Just as a I began to deepen the kiss, Griffin pulled away with a gasp and pushed me off of him.

Rolling from the couch, he jumped up. "I'm so sorry. I didn't mean to do that. The beers I had must have gone to my head. That was stupid. Seriously, I'm so sorry. It meant nothing. Just a mistake."

My heart clenched before shattering into pieces. The dream had been so close, but I lost it. I shook my head as I stood in front of him. "No harm, no foul. Just like messing around when we were sixteen. Chalk it up to horny curiosity." I forced a smile.

Griffin nodded. "I can't let anything mess up what we have. It would kill me to lose you."

"Same." I faked a yawn. "I think I'm going to wash this makeup off and head to bed." I turned and walked to the bathroom again.

The hot water did nothing to ease the ache in my chest or the throbbing in my cock. Once I'd soaped up and rinsed off the makeup, I took my dick in my fist and began to stroke. I leaned one elbow against the tiled wall and imagined Griffin's full, pink lips closed around my thrusting cock. His painted eyes watching me and watching my cock slide between his lips. Imaginary Griffin gripped my ass and took me deeper, so deep he gagged. I squeezed my cock tightly and bit my arm as I came in thick ropes against the shower wall.

Later, I settled into bed and pulled up the original

Peter Pan on my computer. I paid the fee to watch it and donned my headphones.

An hour and twenty minutes later, I dried my tears as I removed the headphones and pushed my computer to the side. I stared at the ceiling with the most amazing and heartbreaking quote from *Peter Pan* floating in my head. *"I'll hold you in my heart until I can hold you in my arms."* But would the time ever come when I could hold Griffin in my arms? Or would he forever remain only in my heart?

Another quote from the movie ghosted through my mind. *"Wait for me somewhere between reality and all we've ever dreamed."* Would my reality ever include Griffin as more than just my friend? Would my dream of loving him as *more* ever become a reality?

I KNEW what Aaron was going to ask even before he opened his mouth.

"You want to go out tonight?"

Aaron was in one of my classes and we'd worked on a short project together with a couple other classmates. He was a good-looking guy, no question. Had a great sense of humor and kept the whole group laughing. I'd been getting vibes from him for a few weeks, so I wasn't shocked when he asked.

He wasn't Griffin.

But Griffin didn't want me.

Or maybe he did, but he refused to mess anything up with our friendship.

Would Grif care if I started dating?

Would it make him jealous?

I nodded and faked a smile. "Sure. What do you have planned?"

Aaron beamed. "Dinner, drinks, then back to your place?"

I hesitated.

"My roommate is having a party, so my place is off limits." Aaron gave a slight shrug.

"Dinner and drinks. My place if we're both up for it." I didn't know if taking Aaron back to my room was a good idea or the worst I'd ever had.

"It's a plan." Aaron slapped me on the back. "Meet me in the quad around six?"

"Sounds good."

That's how I found myself getting dressed for a date on Friday night as a grumpy Griffin quizzed me.

"Where are you going all fancied up?" Grif crossed both arms over his chest.

"Guy in my class asked me to dinner and drinks." I fought the urge to tell Grif I'd cancel if he would just ask.

"What's his name?"

"Aaron."

Grif jutted his chin. "Is he cute?"

I grunted. "He's not ugly."

"How nice." Griffin turned away and went to his room.

I finished my hair and followed him. "What's wrong?"

"Nothing."

"Do you want me to cancel?"

Grif rolled his eyes. "Why would I want you to cancel your date with the not ugly Aaron? I don't own you. You owe me nothing."

I huffed. "Okay. You okay if we come back here later?"

Griffin's eyes bugged and he clenched his jaw. Taking a deep breath, he gritted out. "No, that's fine. I'll be sure to put on my headphones and shut my door."

"You sure?"

Griffin gave me a strange smile. "Yep." He popped the *p* loudly. "Can you close the door behind you? I'm going to turn on a movie. Be safe. Love you."

My heart clenched. "Always. Love you, too." I sighed and closed Grif's door as I left to meet Aaron.

* * *

FOUR HOURS LATER, I patted my pocket for my suite key. "Shit, I must have left my key inside."

"Do you think you lost the key in my car?" Aaron asked.

"Maybe."

"Want to check? Or just knock?"

Trek back to Aaron's car or knock and summon Grif? "Yeah, let's check. I don't want to piss off my roomie."

We went back down the hall and waited for the elevator.

"Your roommate easy to piss off?"

I smiled. "Nah, Griffin is pretty easy going. I just don't want to bother him, plus I'll need that key eventually."

As we exited the elevator, we stopped when a girl in a green staff shirt met us. "Hey! Any chance one of you is looking for a lost key?"

"For real? Yeah, I am," I answered the nighttime lobby attendant.

"Awesome." She dangled the key in front of me. "I wasn't looking forward to trying to figure out who dropped it."

"Where was it?"

"Outside the main door. Some guy turned it in."

"Excellent." I took the key and then Aaron and I waited for the elevator to return.

"Well, that was easier than I thought it would be."

"Definitely. Damn, glad someone found it."

When we reached my room, I unlocked the door and we entered quietly.

"Well, look what the cat dragged in." Griffin piped from the kitchen as he ate a bowl of cereal.

I jerked. "Shit, Grif, I didn't know you were awake."

"Awake. That's me." He took a big bite before asking with his mouth full of cereal, "How were dinner and drinks? Everything you'd dreamed of them to be?"

I rolled my eyes. "Dinner was good. Drinks were good."

Aaron coughed.

"Shit, sorry." I gestured between Aaron and Griffin. "Aaron, my roommate, Griffin. Grif, this is Aaron."

"Nice to meet you." Aaron gave a wave.

"Likewise." Griffin nodded. He turned and poured the rest of his cereal down the disposal. "You two have a blast. Wrap it before you tap it and all." He didn't even glance my way as he beelined toward his room.

"Not easily pissed, huh?" Aaron smirked.

"Not usually."

"He got a thing for you or something?"

"Nah, we're best friends. He's actually my adopted brother."

"Complicated." Aaron raised his brow.

"How so?"

"He clearly has feelings for his best friend slash adopted brother."

I shook my head. "No, we've both agreed that our friendship is first. Always."

"Makes sense to the brain, not so much to the heart."

I gestured toward my room. "Want to watch a movie or something?"

We cozied up on my bed and within minutes Aaron's mouth was on mine. His lips were soft and full, his body hard and warm, and his hands roamed my body in ways that should have lit me on fire.

But he wasn't Griffin.

And Griffin was—what was Griffin? —hurt? Angry?

"Maybe we should call it a night?" Aaron was

already standing from the bed and reaching for the doorknob.

I ran a hand over my face. "Sorry. Griffin was just weird. I'm kinda worried about him."

"He's got it bad for you." Aaron cocked his head. "And I'm thinking the feeling is very much reciprocated."

I kept quiet and walked him to the door. "Thanks for dinner and drinks. Be safe. See you in class."

Aaron kissed my cheek.

I closed the door and frowned.

I turned off the lights and shuffled to my room. Walking through the bathroom, I was determined to ask Grif what the hell had crawled up his butt and why he was acting so shitty.

Griffin was asleep. His features illuminated by the soft glow of his desk lamp. Part of me wanted to shake him awake and ask him what his deal was. Instead, I slipped into his bean bag chair and curled up with my head resting on my elbow. He was so beautiful, so peaceful, and so delicate. Yet I knew he could chew me up and spit me out if he was angry with me. My heart ached with want for the man in front of me. Never would I purposely screw up our friendship, but the desire I had to make Grif more than my best friend was like a freight train roaring through my veins. I wanted him in my arms. I wanted to be in his bed. I wanted our hearts to add *lover* to the list of ways we were connected.

Griffin breathed deeply and shifted in his sleep and I

froze. When he rolled over, I stood slowly and walked to the edge of his bed. Heart hammering in my chest, I leaned down and feathered a kiss against Grif's temple.

"I'll hold you in my heart until I can hold you in my arms."

* * *

"SURPRISED YOU'RE AWAKE." Griffin curled his nose as he studied me head to toe. "Figured you'd be worn out after last night's activities. Did Aaron not keep you *occupied?*"

"He's not here. Had to take off." I realized quickly that Griffin didn't know Aaron had left so early last night. Should I tell him that Aaron and I didn't hook up? Maybe it was better if Griffin thought something happened. Keep us on the friend side of things and temper my crazy thoughts about us ever becoming more.

"He looked just your type."

"What exactly do you think is my *type?*" I bristled, ready to defend myself.

"Well, let's see. Your best friend is a delicate pansy twink who loves makeup and dance and Disney movies. So, pretty much the exact opposite of me, I'd suppose." Griffin leaned against the counter with his arms crossed over his chest.

"You're my best friend, clearly you're somehow my *type.*"

"No, we're exact opposites."

"I'm not arguing. I don't make mistakes when I make friends. Stop putting yourself down." I poured myself some juice. "Do you want to do something tonight?" I knew Griffin was bent out of shape, but I also knew that nothing ever sounded better than spending time with him. "Pizza? Movies? Video games?"

"Nah, count me out. Maybe ask *Aaron* out again. Or head to the local gay bar and see if you can find some willing jocks to get your rocks off." Griffin's cheeks pinked as his angry words flowed.

"So according to you, I'm shallow, dumb, and can only attract a certain segment of the population? Nice." I hated fighting with Grif, but he was in rare form that morning.

He simply jutted his jaw and batted his lashes. "If the shoe fits," he drawled.

"What are you going to do tonight?"

"My usual pathetic homework, Disney movies, and tears. *That* is the type of guy I am." Griffin narrowed his eyes as if to challenge me.

"That doesn't sound like a bad evening at all." I took my glass to the sink and placed a hand on Grif's shoulder. "Stop with the type stuff, Grif. Give me some credit. I'm able to choose my own friends and dates. And I chose you almost a decade ago. Your pity party isn't going to convince me we aren't a perfect match. Plus, we're brothers, so there's no escaping it."

Griffin huffed and jerked his arm away from my touch. "Whatever. Be quiet when you come in tonight.

I'd rather not have to deal with whichever flavor of the day you bring home."

I gathered my things for practice and class with a heavy heart. I didn't like leaving things awkward and tense with Griffin, but I wasn't sure how to fix whatever had gone awry.

6

GRIFFIN

"I NEVER EXPECTED that you could have a broken heart and love with it too, so much that it does not seem broken at all." The quote from *Peter Pan* flitted through my mind the entire day. My heart hurt with wanting Quincy. But I loved him so much I'd never risk our friendship. I just wanted to go back to what we'd had before. Forget the mutual hand jobs. Forget the unexpected kiss. Forget how badly my heart and body wanted Quincy to love me as more than his brother and friend.

But how?

I thought back to how badly it stung to see Q bring *Aaron* home. Maybe he had the right idea. Not that Quincy needed to *get over* me, but maybe moving on, finding someone to distract me, someone to capture my heart in the same way Quincy had would be best for me.

By the late afternoon, I was still in a funk.

I yanked open the coffee shop door and stalked inside with hopes of a sweet, frou-frou drink brightening my mood.

Fifteen minutes later, I sat at a small table sipping my caffeinated goodness and munching on a cookie. The treats tasted good, but I was still grumpy.

"This seat taken?" A hulking guy winked down at me.

"Oh, um," I stuttered, not really sure how to answer. "Feel free, but I'm in a terrible mood and planning to leave soon."

The man sat and smiled. "Nah, don't leave. How will I get to know you if you leave me all alone?"

I recognized his teasing and loosened up a bit. Sipping my drink, I smiled. "Maybe I can stay for a bit."

"My name is David." He held his hand out.

"Griffin." I shook his hand. "You go to school here?"

"Yeah, I'm a junior in Criminal Justice." David held my hand slightly longer than was necessary. "What about you?"

"Freshman business major and cosmetology."

David frowned. "We have a cosmetology department?"

I chuckled. "No, I'm majoring in business here and getting my cosmetology license locally."

"Wow, that's impressive. Will the license take four years?"

"No, I'll get the license within two years. Then I can work at a salon building up my customer base while I finish my business degree." A proud tingle warmed my heart. I knew my plan was somewhat unconventional and lofty, but it was my way out of my past and making it on my own.

"Damn, here I thought I was doing well not flunking any classes." David laughed before sipping his iced drink. "You got plans this evening?"

"Um, what?"

"Plans? Do you have any? If not, maybe we get to know each other a little better?"

I swallowed thickly. "Oh, um..." I didn't really have plans. But I didn't know this guy at all.

"My place is kinda out, I've got three roommates and they all have people over right now."

My mind immediately went to Quincy. What would he think if I brought a complete stranger home? Would his heart clench as much as mine did when he brought Aaron home?

"I've got some studying to do, but we could hang at my place for a while." My heart pounded in my chest. David was attractive and friendly. Hanging out with someone wasn't against any rules. Nothing physical had to happen. I wasn't completely against anything physical. I also wasn't against having a friend. Maybe David could be that for me.

"Sounds good. You close enough to walk?" David finished his drink and stood.

"Yeah, just a couple blocks." I hefted my book bag on my shoulder and led the way out the door.

We made small talk on the walk and reached Green Hall in about ten minutes.

As we rode up the elevator, I thought about Quincy. "I'm not sure if my roommate will be home."

"He cool?"

"Yeah, actually he's my very best friend. And my adopted brother. So, yeah, he's cool." I shrugged. I always found it difficult to try to put into words what Quincy was to me. Best friend. Foster brother turned adopted brother. Those were the easier descriptions. Throw in the years of everything else between Q and me, and it got more complicated.

"Wow, sounds like you've got quite the history." David followed me into the suite.

"We do. Met when we were ten. Pretty much been inseparable since." I tossed my backpack on the floor. "You want a soda or anything?" My heart sagged a bit when I realized Quincy wasn't home.

"Nah, thanks. I'm good. Can I use the bathroom?"

I directed David to our small bathroom and quickly tried to straighten up the living room while he was out of sight.

The toilet flushed and David appeared a few moments later. "This place is great. These two towers were under construction when I was a freshman. Our flat is over in the quad and is big enough for several occupants. But these smaller ones are super. Can I see the bedrooms? I wonder if a buddy and I could get one of these for next year."

I swung the door open to my room. "The suites really are nice. Like apartment living, but on campus and close to everything."

David stood in the middle of my room and whistled. "You really don't know how good you've got it here, man. New place, great rooms, lots of space."

The door clicking closed took me by surprise and my heart leapt into my throat.

Suddenly David looked very large, very imposing, and very dangerous.

"Um, what's up?" I stuttered. "Thought we'd sit in the living room. It's more comfortable."

"Nah, I like it here," David mumbled as he advanced on me. He didn't stop until my ass hit the desk. "Private."

What the fuck had happened? One moment I was thinking, *I'm making a friend with an upper classman,* and the next moment I'm trying to figure out how I'll get away from him.

"I'd rather go out to the living room." I tried to bypass David.

"I'd rather not. How about a little kiss?" David blocked my escape.

Two things happened at that moment. The first was I looked to my right and saw a thick stack of books I'd been using for studying. The second thing was I heard the front door open and my knees nearly buckled in relief. Quincy was home. While I definitely *would* clobber this asshole David with a book to the head, I breathed easier knowing Q was there to support me.

I took a deep breath. "I'm going to ask you one more time to please move and let me by," I spoke through gritted teeth.

"Nah, we're just getting to know each other. Let's see where this thing goes."

With a sudden movement, I stretched both arms to my right and clutched the top book on the stack. As I swung the book toward David's head with all of the force I could muster, I screamed, "I said, *no!*" The book connected with David's temple with a satisfying thud and the man stumbled away from me, holding his head.

The bedroom door flew open, and Quincy rushed in as David moaned, his hands cradling his head. "G, you okay?" Quincy demanded.

"What the *fuck*, Griffin?" David cried out. "Oh God, I think I'm going to pass out."

"Oh, you're going *out,* all right. Out of this room, this suite, and this college if I have anything to say about it." I shoved David toward the bedroom door knowing Quincy was right by my side.

"Griffin, come on. Let's talk about this." David pleaded as he lumbered through the living room. "It was a misunderstanding."

"You put me in an uncomfortable position. I asked you to stop. You continued making me feel awkward." I pushed David's shoulder again, glad he was near the door.

"Then you got bitch slapped by a business book." Quincy grabbed David's arm and thrust him toward the door.

"There was no misunderstanding." I opened the door and allowed Q to toss David into the hallway. "Q, can you watch him while I call security?"

Quincy's nostrils flared as he nodded.

Once the dorm security officer arrived and took my statement along with David's information, I was beginning to lose steam.

Security assured David would be banned from Green Hall and the report would be submitted to campus police as well as the criminal justice department.

Quincy and I walked back into the suite.

I shuffled toward the kitchen as Quincy slid the chain and dead bolt into place. After downing a glass of water, I stood at the sink braced on my arms, taking big gulping breaths.

Quincy's arms wrapped around me. "Are you okay?"

I shuddered. "Physically, yes. Just scared." My breaths had slowed the moment Quincy took me in his arms. "Feeling really stupid right now."

"Who the hell was that? Why was he here?"

"Can I take a shower first?" I needed the hot water to help relax me.

"Of course. I'll get us some food." Q hugged me closer before directing me toward the bathroom.

By the time I emerged, I was feeling mostly better. Overall, I was pissed at myself and beyond angry at David.

Quincy hollered from his room. "In here, Grif."

After pulling on sleep pants and a t-shirt, I ran a towel through my damp hair once more before traveling back through the steamy bathroom to Q's room.

"Come on." Quincy patted the bed. "We've got sushi and movies."

I climbed into his bed and settled in.

Quincy handed me a plastic container of sushi.

"Did you go get this?"

"Delivery. You can get practically anything delivered on a college campus." He bumped my shoulder and let me take a few bites. "You want to tell me what happened?"

I sighed. "It all sounds so stupid now."

"That's okay. I want to hear it." Quincy turned on a movie and *The Many Adventures of Winnie the Pooh* began to play.

"So, I was in a terrible mood. That David guy asked if he could sit with me at the coffee shop." I huffed. "In retrospect, I should have recognized he came on much too strong, but I was completely out of sorts. When he suggested we come back to my room, I wasn't really thinking of anything but hanging out." I shook my head with my eyes closed. "I'm so glad you came home, Q."

"Grif, you bashed that guy's head. You had it under control." Quincy put his arm around me. "But I'm glad I came home too."

"I did hit him pretty hard." I chuckled. "Thank goodness for that big ol' stack of books."

"And here I thought studying was useless," Q teased.

We finished our sushi and settled in to watch the rest of the movie.

"You know what this movie teaches?" I mumbled, barely able to keep my eyes open as the movie came to an end.

"What?"

"Close friends are life's greatest treasures. Cherish your time together."

"I cherish every moment with you, Grif," Quincy whispered.

7

QUINCY

I WOKE with Grif in my arms, and I never wanted to wake any other way from that day on. He was curled into my chest, my arms wrapped around him, our legs tangled, and our groins nearly mashed together. I breathed him in, savoring his warmth and the press of his body against mine.

Griffin wiggled, shifting in my arms slightly with a murmur and groan.

And his hard cock brushed mine.

Fuck. I was done. I tensed in an attempt to stop my cock from growing even harder, but it was no use. Grif's morning wood laid parallel to my own, and my body begged to thrust into him. I nearly broke something I gritted my jaw so tight.

I knew the moment Grif realized where he was. He stirred again, stretching slightly, nuzzling his nose into my chest, and pressing his cock into mine.

And then he froze, stiff as a board in my arms.

Did he realize I was awake? Maybe I could pretend to be asleep.

And then my beautiful best friend mumbled and acted as if he was sleep talking as he gently pulled his hips from mine.

Okay, Grif. We can play that way.

I moaned as if in the middle of a dream and rolled my hips so that our dicks touched again.

I kept my eyes closed, and I knew Grif's were shut, as well.

But he totally played the part of horny sleeping guy and wriggled, thrust, and moaned as he kept up the dream act. It was an act, right? I was almost one hundred percent sure he was awake.

How far were either of us willing to take this little charade?

I'd given Grif a hand job back when we were sixteen, so was an early morning frottage session over the line?

What if the rutting was done by two guys pretending to be asleep?

Yeah, probably a little too far. If we couldn't thrust our cocks together while admitting we were fully awake, we probably shouldn't be doing it.

I jerked as if I'd just woken up and rolled from Grif slowly.

"Oh, hey," Grif mumbled as if he'd just woken up. "What time is it? I should go to my own bed."

"Pretty sure it's morning."

"Shit, I'm sorry. I didn't mean to sleep here all night." Grif groaned and shifted away from me.

My body immediately screamed for his warm touch to return. "No worries."

Griffin climbed from my bed, attempting and failing to hide his dick tenting his pants. "Better get a shower and some food. I'm going to clean and study today."

I turned over just enough that I *hoped* my hard-on was hidden. "Yeah, sounds good. I'll hit the gym. Maybe dinner tonight?"

Grif nodded as he inched toward the bathroom.

"Hey, you okay? After last night and everything?"

His brows drew together for a split second as if he'd forgotten David. "Oh, yeah. I'm good. Thanks for taking care of me."

"Always."

And then Grif retreated to the bathroom.

The second I heard the door lock and the shower turn on, my hand shot to my throbbing dick and began to stroke. I imagined Grif's pretty pink lips on my shaft, his tongue licking my slit, and my tongue teasing his hole.

The thump and moan I heard from the bathroom distracted me for a second.

Holy shit. Was Grif jacking off?

Was he thinking about me? No way. Griffin had made it clear he wasn't willing to mess up our friendship for some sex experiment. What if we messed around more than we already had and it wasn't good and then things were awkward between us? I agreed with Grif, nothing was worth losing our friendship.

But my warped and greedy mind didn't stop imagining my best friend on his knees swallowing my cock until I shot my load all over my hand.

I grabbed a tissue and wiped myself. Sighing, I flopped back onto my pillow. Waking with Grif in my arms was amazing. But it didn't mean anything. Right? We'd slept so close to each other for so many years, it just made sense we'd cuddle up when a smaller bed pushed us so close together.

Yeah, nothing wrong with cuddling.

But I had to get myself under control. I wanted Griffin and not just sexually. But there was way too much history between us and I wasn't willing to risk our friendship. And what if I asked Griffin to take things to the next step and he turned me down? It was better to just keep my best friend.

"GRIFFIN, Momma will kill Dad and I if you don't come to Thanksgiving."

Grif screwed up his face. "I don't know. Feels like it should just be a family thing, I don't want to be third wheel."

I closed my eyes and drew in a deep breath as I rubbed my temples. "Griffin Murphy-Sanders, that's your name, right?"

Grif scowled as he stood from the kitchen table to rinse his cereal bowl. "Yes?"

"You hear the *Sanders* part in there?"

Grif rolled his eyes. "I know I'm technically your family. At least on paper. But that was when I was a little kid who couldn't take care of myself. I'm grown. It feels like Momma and Pops have put in their time with me. You and Max should go and enjoy the holiday."

"You know, for a smart guy, you're really acting dumb right now." I moved so that Grif's back was in the corner of the countertop. I pinned him in, my hands on the counter on either side of his waist. Oh God, I was so close I could smell his fresh scent, feel his heat. His eyes were wide. Was I imagining the fire in them? Wishful thinking on my part? Every part of my being wanted to kiss him. Instead, I swallowed and spoke low and clear. "You *are* family. You *are* their son. You *are* my brother in every way that matters. Even if we'd only grown up as friends, I'd expect you at our Thanksgiving." Not trusting myself completely, I took a risk and pulled Grif into a hard hug. "I need you with me. They want you there. This shouldn't even be a discussion. Say you'll come." My words were gruff at his ear.

Grif was quiet and still for a while, but he eventually wrapped his arms around my waist and whispered, "Yeah, Q. I'll come with you."

I sagged with relief. Partly because I couldn't imagine Thanksgiving without him. Mostly because he'd just saved me from Momma's wrath. "Thank you.

Please don't ever doubt that you're expected, invited, wanted, and loved. Always." My voice shook more than I meant for it to.

Grif shuddered in my arms. "Yeah, okay. Thanks for the reminder."

"We'll leave after classes tomorrow. You're done early, right?" I stepped away from him slightly.

Grif nodded. "Yeah, I should be able to leave by noon. What about you?"

"About the same. Let's shoot for noon, maybe one."

* * *

"So, Dad has the stomach flu. He's not going." I said as I disconnected from my dad.

"Bummer. He okay? It's just the flu?" Grif tossed his duffle toward the door.

"Yeah, but he's been puking all day. Doesn't want to risk giving it to anyone. Plus, the drive would be a bitch." Dad was close enough to drive to Momma and Pops', but it would have been a sucky drive while sick.

"Yeah, that sucks."

By the time we reached Momma and Pops' house, Griffin and I had listened to our favorite tunes, laughed about old memories, and talked about the classes we would be wrapping up this semester.

Momma and Pops were waiting on the porch.

"Did you tell them what time we were coming?" Grif glanced my way.

I chuckled. "No, seems they just know these things. Momma does at least. She's a badass."

"Truth."

We grabbed our bags and rushed up the stairs to find ourselves wrapped in warm hugs and cheek kisses.

"You boys look wonderful. We've been so excited about you coming home. Shame Max is sick, but we'll make the best of it." Momma ushered us into the house. "I've got your old room all set up. Get settled in and then come to the kitchen to help me with tomorrow's dinner preparations." She led us to our old bedroom.

I couldn't help the smile and the pitter-patter of my heart when I saw our beds were still pushed together. "You kept them together?" I glanced at Griffin.

He shrugged. "Gave me a bigger bed."

"I don't have the heart to separate them," Momma explained. "Every time I see those beds side-by-side I'm reminded of the night you two put them together and the friendship that took root then and there. Warms my heart." She stood between us and put and arm around both of us. "Brotherhood, friendship, and so much more was born in this room."

My cheeks flamed at the *so much more*. Surely she wasn't insinuating anything. Right?

Griffin cleared his throat. "Great memories here for sure."

Momma kissed us both on the cheek again and turned to go downstairs. "I'll be in the kitchen. Come down when you're settled."

Griffin and I walked to the bed and tossed our bags on the floor.

"Wow, it's not changed at all." I glanced around the room.

"I never felt like I could change it after you left. Not that there was anything I would have changed, but it only felt right to keep it the same." Griffin moved toward the window. "I can't believe Pops knew about the porn and moonshine."

I laughed loudly. "Better him than Momma."

"We were so stupid."

"The moonshine was stupid. The porn was normal."

Grif's gaze caught mine and we froze. "Do you regret it?" His words were barely audible.

My heart leaped to my throat. "Not for a single second."

"Boys, I could use a hand down here," Momma hollered up the stairs.

The moment was broken and we quickly tramped down to the kitchen.

* * *

"Now, Quincy, you make sure you're only taking off the peeling of those potatoes. See how Griffin's apple peelings are paper thin? That's what your pile of potato peelings should look like."

"Yes, Momma." I bumped my hip against Griffin's. "Always trying to be as perfect as Grif."

He bumped me back. "It's a lofty goal."

"When you're finished with those, I want you to roll out the pie crusts and get them in the pans. The fillings are mostly ready to go in. Griffin, you'll need to finish the apple pie filling when you finish with those apples." Momma checked on the greens and corn in pots on the stove. "I'll get the macaroni and cheese laid out in the pan so I can just bake it tomorrow."

"You've got the grits, right?" I asked even though I knew there was no way Momma would skip the grits. It was tradition.

"Of course. And fried chicken for Griffin." Momma patted Grif's shoulder.

I chuckled. "Anything for Griffin. Griffin doesn't like turkey. Griffin gets fried chicken. Spoiled brat."

Griffin gave a cheeky smile. "Turkey is dry and tasteless. Fried chicken is juicy and tasty and of God."

"If Griffin likes my fried chicken better than turkey, I'll make it for him every time." Momma flicked my ear. "But, boy, you better never blaspheme my turkey like that. Just because you prefer fried chicken doesn't mean my turkey is *dry* or *tasteless*." She flicked Grif's ear too.

"Yes, Momma," we answered in unison.

"You have any kids right now?" Griffin began mixing cinnamon, sugar, and lemon juice with the bowl apple chunks.

"Not right now. We had two sisters for a few months. Just long enough for their parents to get settled into new jobs and find a decent place to live. We've started taking in a lot of kids like that. The parents aren't doing anything wrong, but we take the kids for a while so the parents can get settled and save up some money so they don't end up having issues with the courts." Momma bustled around the kitchen. "Had three boys before the sisters. Those three boys were heartbreaking. One of them got to go back to his momma, and I really think it was for the best. The other two were adopted. 'Course, they were little. Those little ones are always snatched up so quick. Never understand why anyone wants to deal with diapers and toddlers when they could get an older kid." She wrapped an arm around Grif's shoulders and hugged him close.

My heart fluttered when he melted into her.

"They all come from bad trauma?" Grif whispered and I knew he was remembering his own parents and trauma.

"The one who got to go back to his mom was the least affected. She'd been selling drugs. He was in foster care while she got her CNA license. Now that she's making legal money, the courts feel she can care for him. The grandma lives with them so she can watch him when Mom is at work. He's school-aged. I met the mom; I think they are in a better situation now."

I poured cherry pie filling into the pie crust. Not the canned filling; Momma would die before using that. I was talking real pie cherries, the red-tart pitted kind. "The other boys have it worse?"

Momma rubbed her chest before dabbing her eyes with her apron. "Oh, those poor babies. Malnourished, broken bones, locked in dark closets, and burned in hot water baths." She shuddered. "Maybe two of the most traumatized little ones I've ever seen."

I didn't even think when I heard Grif gasp. I put my arm around him and pulled him close.

"Brothers?" I asked, not taking my arm from Grif's shoulders.

"Yes, two-years-old and three-years-old. Different fathers from what I was told. One of the fathers is incarcerated. The other was part of the abuse. Both the mom and that father are in jail right now. But based on the history and severity of abuse, both have lost their rights to the children. The boys were adopted by a beautiful couple from California. Two dads, great jobs, one works from home, already had an amazing nanny lined up with a great family support system. I think those boys will end up just fine. More than fine."

"It's always good when a kid gets the perfect forever family," Griffin whispered.

I nearly lost it. I put my lips against the top of his head almost as if I was kissing his head. "The forever family wins in that case too."

Griffin took a shaky breath and moved from my arms to add some pieces of butter to the pie he was working on before covering it with the top crust and cutting slits in the crust to vent it for baking.

As the preparations drew to a close, Momma washed her hands and surveyed the kitchen. "Well, boys, it looks like we've done as much as possible for now. Thank you for your help. Who's in the mood for a game?"

"Yes!" Griffin whooped and rushed from the kitchen only to return with the Disney edition of Trivial Pursuit™.

"Oh Lord, we may as well all prepare to have our asses handed to us."

"On a platter," Grif agreed with a swish of his hips and a twirl as he left the room to set up the game.

Two hours later, Grif had won two games and my cheeks hurt from smiling so much. I wasn't a master of Disney like Griffin, but having him, Momma, and Pops by my side while we all laughed and joked was quite possibly one of the best things on earth.

"Well, I'm thoroughly beaten and ready for bed." Pops stood and stretched. "Good to have you boys home. Sleep tight." Pops shuffled from the room. I recognized at that moment that he seemed a lot older than when I'd last been home. Pops wasn't a big man, but he'd always been larger than life in his quiet supportive ways. It gave me pause to realize he was aging.

"I'm going to check the kitchen, then I'll be up." Momma stood and kissed us both before bustling off to the kitchen.

"Does that woman ever stop?" Grif mused.

"Not that I've ever seen."

Griffin gathered up the game before we headed up the stairs.

"You tired?" I asked.

"Tired, yes. Sleepy, no."

"Want to watch a movie?"

"Yeah. You can choose, but you have to do it my way." Griffin grinned.

"Is *your way* telling me the movie you want to watch?"

"No, it's fair." Griffin grabbed an old tie from the closet.

"Oh, kinky," I teased.

"Shut up." He tied it around my eyes and maneuvered me to the DVD shelf. He spun me five times and then told me to reach out and pick a movie.

I stumbled to the right, but Grif caught me and held me steady. I reached for the shelf, running my hand along the DVD cases a couple times before picking one.

"Yes!" Griffin crowed. "Disney for the win."

I yanked the tie from my face and rolled my eyes. "That shelf is ninety percent Disney, of course it won. What did I pick?"

Griffin smiled and waved *Peter Pan* in front of my face.

I shook my head and chuckled. "Well then, let's get it started."

Grif and I settled into bed propped against pillows, our shoulders, hips, and thighs touching.

After watching most of the movie with Grif whispering much of the dialogue, my eyes began to flutter shut. As the golden ship took to the sky and floated across the screen, I slipped into a pleasant sleep knowing Griffin was in my bed and by my side.

I had the most amazing dream. Griffin was in my

arms, he wanted to be with me, we were a couple and everything was perfect. We were content and happy.

And then I woke up and Griffin really was in my arms. He was warm, cuddled in my embrace, his nose nuzzled against my chest. I wanted this every day for the rest of my life. Without thinking, I ran my hand down Grif's back.

He tensed and I knew he was awake.

A thousand thoughts ran through my mind.

"Grif." My voice was horse.

"Yeah?" He whispered.

My heart thundered like I'd run a marathon. "What if... what if what we *think* is our reality is actually keeping us from all we've ever dreamed?" I held my breath in anticipation.

"I'm dreaming, right? Waking in your arms while you philosophize with *Peter Pan* quotes *has* to be a damn dream." Griffin's words were gravely and he wriggled in my arms.

I took his answer as encouragement. He didn't flinch being in my arms. He didn't gasp and try to get away. He didn't tell me I was being ridiculous. Yet. So, I continued.

"You mean more to me than anyone in this whole world." I murmured the words against his head.

"More Peter Pan? You're pulling out the big guns." Griffin's smile was evident in his voice. "What do you want me to say, Q?"

"I'm tired of waiting on you between our reality and all we've ever dreamed." Okay, I was likely running the

Pan quotes into the ground, but it helped me say what I wanted to say.

"I never asked you to wait. You don't have to wait for me. Where is all of this coming from?"

"That's not the point. I'll always wait for you. And this isn't new; I've wanted more with you probably since that jack-off session way back when. You and me, G. It's the only thing that makes sense to me. But I'm ready to stop waiting. I want to change our reality. I want those dreams."

Griffin was silent for several moments before he sighed. "But our reality is good. What if our dreams can't match what we have?"

"But what if they *can*?" I rested my hand on Grif's lower back and pulled him close. "Why don't we jump? Take the chance? Let this happen?"

Grif shook his head against my chest. "It's our history. There's so much against us. We're foster brothers, you're private school versus me being public, you're sporty while I'm Disney, dancing, and makeup."

"And I've loved those differences from the first day I met you." I rubbed his back.

"You did *not* love everything about me from day one," Griffin argued.

"Okay, maybe not day *one*. But not long after. At least from the night we pushed these beds together."

"I'm your grandparents' adopted son. How are you going to explain our relationship if we get together?" Griffin continued to voice his concerns.

"Tell the fuckers I've got a hot-ass brother and dare

them to say something about it?" I laughed and hugged Grif tight. "I'll respect your choice if you are adamant about not taking a chance on us. But I need you to know I want something more with you. I love you and that will never change."

"But what if we don't work? I can't lose you." Grif's words wavered.

"You've had me since we were ten years old. No matter what happens, you'll always be my brother and my best friend." I pushed him from me so I could tip up his chin and see his eyes. "I think what we have could explode into something amazing, what dreams are made of, a forever type thing."

"Forever?" Griffin squeaked.

"You're stuck with me forever either way. I figure we might as well see how things go with adding another layer to our relationship. If it doesn't work, we go back to being only brothers and best friends. But think about how awesome it would be to go from two B's to three B's." I raised a brow and grinned.

"Three B's?"

"Brothers, besties, *and* boyfriends."

"I'm pretty sure those three words aren't usually put together." Griffin shook his head but he smiled.

"Yeah well, we've always been unique. Why stop now?"

Griffin cuddled back into my chest. "So how would it work? Just boom we're boyfriends?"

"Nah, I'm thinking we could flirt and mess around, take things slow and see how we're feeling about it. If it's weird to mess around, we'll call it quits." I breathed softly against his ear. "But I remember that night in this bed." My lips brushed his ear. "I remember that kiss." I pushed my hips into him. "I don't think it's going to be weird at all."

Griffin groaned. "Okay. Can I think about it? Maybe take a shower to clear my head?"

I nodded. "I'm not going to be mad if you say no. I'll be sad because I want you in my arms and my bed, but you'll never not be in my heart, so it's all good."

Griffin nodded and rolled from the bed.

"YOU AND GRIFFIN seem to be doing very well." Momma stood at the kitchen counter stirring up what I assumed was pancake batter. No one made buttermilk pancakes like Momma. She'd ruined me for all other pancakes.

I narrowed my eyes. What was she insinuating? "Yeah, we've settled in well. It's great to be back together. I loved spending so much time with Dad, but I missed Grif like crazy."

"Mmhm." Momma hummed as she added the final touches to the batter. Then she flicked some water on the griddle. As it sizzled, she smiled over her shoulder at me. "Perfect. Come help me with these pancakes. You pour. I'll flip."

I smiled. Making pancakes with Momma had been a favorite childhood memory. It usually involved whichever foster kids were staying with us at the time, but I loved when Momma would pull a stool to the counter and let all of us kids take turns pouring the batter, and practice flipping the pancakes. I poured three connected circles in a Mickey Mouse shape. "For Grif," I explained.

"I figured," Momma replied dryly. "You know, I knew the moment I stuck the two of you together that you'd have something special. I knew you'd protect him. I knew you'd have a brotherly love. But when that turned into an inseparable friendship, I couldn't have been happier."

"Yeah, I wasn't thrilled sharing my room with him, but it all worked out best in the end. Momma always knows what's she's doing." I bumped my hip against hers.

"And now?" Momma busied herself with flipping the pancake.

"Now? Griffin and I are great. Brothers and best friends always. No worries there." I knew Momma was like a dog with a bone. She had something to ask or say or a point to make. I settled in and waited.

"Pops and I were friends first."

"Yeah, I remember. That's a great story." It really was. I couldn't imagine my grandparents as young kids, but I loved hearing about them growing up as best friends.

"Oh, I used to get so mad at that boy. But he was my very best friend from the very first day he moved next door. We were about five and took to each other like fish to water. When we were older, Pops wanted us to date, but I was worried it would mess things up."

"But it didn't, right?" I knew Griffin and I would be taking a risk, but I also knew I'd never stop loving him or considering him my brother and best friend, so I had concluded that the risk was worth it.

"No, it didn't mess anything up. We were so used to being together and taking care of each other that adding a romance side to it came as easily as breathing." Momma waited for me to pour more batter. "But it doesn't always work out so easily."

"If you knew two best friends were contemplating becoming more than friends, what would your advice be?" I trusted Momma with my life, and I had no issue telling her what was going on with Griffin and me.

She was quiet for a moment. "I'd tell them to respect their original relationship, protect it at all costs, and never stop loving each other. If a romantic relationship is meant to be between best friends then it will feel right, come easy, and be simple." Momma took a deep breath. "The unknown is scary. But the what-could-be has a chance to be so dang amazing, why risk missing out?"

"That's what I'm hoping for." I poured another pancake as Momma removed one.

"And if the relationship was built on trust, friendship, love, and respect then it can withstand an upset if a romance doesn't work out." Momma scooped up the last of the pancakes onto a platter. "What's Griffin thinking about this possible new possibility?"

"I think he's more like young you; I'm more like young Pops."

"Ah, yeah. I can see that. Griffin has had a lot of uncertainty in his life, I'm sure the worry of losing the security of your friendship weighs on him."

"But how do I convince him that I'll never leave him, even if things don't work out romantically?" I swiped a pancake from the platter and smiled when Momma smacked at my hand.

"You gotta be patient. Make a romantic relationship with his best friend so life-altering and fulfilling that he can't resist. And if it peters out, you stay by his side because he'll always be your brother and best friend." Momma kissed my cheek and pulled me into a hug. "Now, go tell Pops and Griffin that breakfast is ready. You can shower after we eat."

I hollered at Pops to come in for breakfast. Momma swatted me with a towel. "I could have done that myself, child." I ran from the kitchen laughing. Once upstairs, I paused outside the bathroom door to tell Grif it was time to eat. Right before I made a smartass comment about saving me some water, I heard Grif's low groan and the sound of something falling. Holy shit. Was Griffin jacking off in the shower?

I leaned against the door and willed my ears to hear more. But the water shut off soon after.

Was he thinking about me? Was waking up in my arms what made him need to rub one out? God, I hoped so.

Lost in thought, I jumped when the bathroom door opened.

Griffin stood there, wrapped in a towel with drippy hair and flushed cheeks. His wide eyes stared at me and his cheeks probably could have started a fire. "What are you doing?" His voice was a cross between a horny husky and a caught-in-the-act squeaky.

I smirked. "Just came to tell you that breakfast is ready."

Griffin swallowed.

My cock jerked as I watched his throat. The steamy warmth of his damp body, the fresh scent of his soap, and the memory of his groan as he came in the shower mixed together to torment me. "So, yeah. Breakfast is ready. Hurry up and come down or the pancakes will be gone."

Grif groaned again. "Pancakes? God, I love Momma's pancakes." He headed toward the bedroom.

"Same and I'm not saving you any." I caught myself before slapping his ass. I wanted to touch him, but I needed to make sure he was onboard. "See you down there."

8

GRIFFIN

I WATCHED as Quincy ate what had to be his eighteenth pancake and smiled when he pushed back from the table and announced he was stuffed.

"Momma, I'm going to shower. You can leave the dishes and Grif and I will take care of them." Q kissed her on top of the head. "Thank you for breakfast."

Momma patted his hand. "You're welcome, baby. Enjoy your shower."

My mind thought back to my shower. My cock had been rock hard from the moment I'd woken up in Quincy's arms. I'd hoped the shower would relieve the issue, but it hadn't. I'd taken my length in a soapy hand and stroked. Quincy's words, his touch, everything about our morning together had come rushing back, and I came harder than I ever had. Hell, I'd even knocked a shampoo bottle off the damn shelf.

And finding Q outside the door almost made me

hyperventilate. Had he heard me? What would he think if he figured out I was jacking off in the shower? Surely he knew I didn't have a ton of experience with intimacy. I couldn't be blamed for jerking off, right? Guys did it all the time. But they weren't often thinking of their brother/best friend.

Quincy wanted more between us. God, I wanted more too. But we were so damn different. And I couldn't stomach the thought of losing my best friend if things didn't work out. Plus, Quincy had a lot more experience than me. I was sure of it. I'd given exactly one blow job in high school and it was a disaster. The guy had offered to return the favor, but I'd been shaking so badly and thinking of Quincy that I told him I was good. I'd had some kisses here and there, but no sexual contact beyond jerking off with Quincy and a poorly executed blow job in high school.

I wasn't ashamed of my lack of experience. I wasn't dying to add to my sexual repertoire just for the sake of adding to it either. And any chances I'd ever had to gain experience were always avoided or turned down. For exactly one reason. Quincy. Anything I'd ever wanted to do always seemed wrong unless it was with Quincy. And none of it could ever be with Quincy.

Right?

"*Griffin.*" Momma stood across the table, hands on hips, saying my name in a way that made me realize I'd totally zoned out.

"Huh? Oh, sorry. I spaced it." I stood and took my plate to the sink.

"Why don't you wash and I'll dry. We need to get lunch cooking. We'll eat around one o'clock since we had a later breakfast." Momma bustled to bring dishes to the sink. "Duane can you put the turkey in. The oven is ready. Bird needs about three and a half hours to bake. I did the macaroni this morning so it just needs kept warm."

Pops nodded and gave Momma a kiss before he set to work removing the turkey from the refrigerator and putting it in the oven.

I ran hot water in the sink and added soap. Momma had a dishwasher, but she preferred doing dishes by hand most of the time. I began to soak the dishes and scrub them while Momma cleared the table.

"Tell me what's new, child. How's school? Are you doing okay with two majors? Any cute boys you're interested in?" Momma's questions poured from her sweet mouth as if she hadn't just put me on the spot. The woman totally knew what she was doing. She could always get me talking.

I rolled my eyes and shrugged while I continued washing a plate. "School is great. Having Quincy there with me is great. I knew I missed having him around, but I didn't realize how much until we were back together. It's like we just have a certain calm around us when we're together. And classes are great. I'm not actually *double* majoring. I'm just majoring in business while also getting my cosmetology license. It's going well. I'm not overwhelmed. At least not at the moment." I rinsed the soapy dishes and moved them to the dish drainer so Momma could dry them.

Pops laughed. "You never were good at evading your Momma's questions, boy." He patted my shoulder. "Might as well tell her about the cute boy who has caught your interest. She'll get it out of you eventually."

My cheeks heated, and I bit my lip. "How do you know there's a cute boy?"

"She's your Momma. She knows it all. And tells me all about it." Pops chuckled again and headed to the living room. "Parade probably already started, but I got it set to record. You and your boy come watch it with me when you're ready."

I blanched and glanced at Momma. "Me and my boy?" My voice squeaked and I contemplated sticking my head in the sink of dishwater.

"Child, Momma always knows. You and Quincy. What's going on with that?" Momma dried a plate and stacked it in a cabinet.

I sighed. "You should work for the FBI or something."

"I'd have to be blind to miss the connection between you two, the subtle looks. You've always had a connection, a kinship, but this is different. I noticed it the moment you two climbed from the car. There's something more. I think you've both been fighting it, avoiding it, hiding from it. But maybe it's time to stop doing that? Face it head-on? What are your thoughts? How are you feeling?" Momma continued drying dishes.

Glad to have dishes remaining in the sink, I busied myself with washing while I spoke. "I'm torn. I'm scared. I'm unsure. That's how I'm feeling. Torn because I've wanted something more with Q since we were sixteen, maybe even before. But I also don't want to mess up what we have. He's my brother, my best friend. I need that. I'm scared I'll lose him if things don't work out between us. And I'm unsure because I don't know that I'm enough for him. He's so much more than me. He's more experienced, more outgoing, and just so much *more*. I'm none of those things." I took a deep breath after spilling my guts.

"Griffin Murphy-Sanders, if I ever hear you put yourself down like that again, I'll take a switch to your behind." Momma stood with her hands on her hips.

I laughed out loud. "You'd never switch a fly."

She smirked. "Okay, you're right about that. But I better never hear you talking down about yourself ever again. Period. You two have been thick as thieves since that stormy night so many years ago. You're opposites in so many ways, but that's part of why you work so well. You've always just clicked. I knew it the moment I dragged you into Quincy's room. That boy loves you, cherishes you, and looks up to you. He's always been your protector and supporter."

"That's just it. He's all those things for me," I started, but Momma cut me off.

"Don't interrupt. He may be all those things to you, but you're that much and more for him. You love him? Cherish him?"

I nodded. "Always."

"You look up to him?"

"Yeah, he's amazing. He's taught me so much."

"You may not be his protector in the physical strength meaning of the word, but you've protected him just as much as he has you. And you've been his strongest supporter all these years. What's more is that you've kept him grounded; you give him reason to be his best. I know that boy wouldn't have done as well in school as he did without your help. You never let him hide who he was; I'm not sure that would have happened if not for you." Momma placed a hand on my shoulder. "You're just as good for him as he is for you. Experiences be damned. Whatever either of you lack, you can teach the other, or learn together."

Like frottage, rimming, and anal? I nearly choked on my tongue as the words ran through my head. I cleared my throat. "Yeah, I can see that. I guess I'm just afraid to mess up what we have."

"How do you know it will mess things up?"

I shrugged. "I don't. But I can't stand the thought of losing him."

"The way I see it, you're brothers and best friends and I don't think either of you will ever let that go. And instead of thinking that it *could* mess things up, why don't you think about the fact that it *could* turn into the best thing ever; the one big love of your life. Forever and always."

"You sound just like Quincy."

Momma beamed. "He's a smart boy."

I nodded and rinsed the last dish. "So, this is one of those sappy take a chance, it could turn into the best thing of your life type things?"

"No sense being afraid when the worst thing that could happen is going back to being brothers and best friends."

"No, the worst thing..." I started but Momma held up a hand.

"Hush. I won't hear of it. You'll either spend the rest of your life as brothers, best friends, and boyfriends, maybe husbands one day, or you'll find out you're better as brothers and best friends. Either way, you're together and loved."

"Did Quincy tell you about the three B's?" I laughed.

"Three B's?"

"Never mind." I waved her off. "Let's go watch the parade."

At that moment, Quincy whooped as he rushed down the stairs. "Parade and football! Gather 'round y'all!"

Pops was dozing in his recliner. Momma took her chair. Quincy and I settled in on opposite ends of the couch with our legs stretched out so we were touching from thigh to feet. Quincy ran his big toe against my leg and winked.

My heart fluttered and I immediately knew that I wanted to jump into whatever Quincy and I might have together. *What if it crashes and burns?* That little voice niggled at my head. *But what if it doesn't? What if it's amazing and forever and always?* I argued back with a smile on my face.

My phone buzzed.

Quincy: *Momma seems to think there's something between us.*

My eyes darted from my phone to Quincy.

He smirked.

Me: *What did you tell her?*

Quincy: *That I've loved you forever and I want to see if we can add another layer.*

Me: *Did you mention the three B's?*

Quincy frowned and shook his head.

I shrugged.

Quincy: *How was your shower?*

My face caught fire.

Me: *Nice. Thanks. Yours?*

Quincy: *Did you think of me while you jacked off? I thought about you.*

My eyes bugged and I glanced around the room. Momma was watching the parade and Pops had dozed off.

Quincy: *I want to hold you, kiss you, and jack you.*

Me: *We've actually done all three of those things. Check them off your list.*

Quincy: *I want to do them again, for real. And do more. If you're okay with it.*

Me: *And if I'm not?*

Quincy pouted but tapped out a message.

Quincy: *I can respect that G. I just feel it in my soul that this could be so much more.*

Me: *Or crash and burn. And then what?*

Quincy: *What would happen if this was one of the movies you love so much?*

I huffed and rolled my eyes as I attempted to fight back a smirk.

Quincy raised a brow.

Me: *The characters would take a chance and they'd live happily ever after.*

Quincy: *Then let's take a chance and live happily ever after.*

I was quiet for several moments.

Me: *I want a contract.*

Quincy: *Ohhh, like something kinky, 50 shades-ish?*

I laughed and shook my head.

Pops snorted and stirred. Momma tutted over a float she thought was *just as pretty as a picture.*

Me: *No, just us saying that we'll give this a shot and if it's not working for one or the other we'll go back to being best friends and brothers only. We won't let it ruin what we have.*

Quincy: *I'm game. But I want an addendum to the contract. I'll write my part up.*

I couldn't help the grin that spread across my face.

Quincy set to work tapping out his addendum while I busied myself with the contract.

Fifteen minutes later, I took one last look at what I'd written. I thought it was sufficient.

We the undersigned do mutually agree to enter into an intimate relationship on the date signed. By mutual agreement, if either party feels uncomfortable in the relationship or decides he wishes to back out, the relationship will immediately return to ONLY adopted brothers and best friends. There will be no weirdness or hurt feelings.

I tossed my phone to Q. "Read it and sign it."

"Bossy." He grinned and handed his phone to me. "Only after you agree to add this."

I narrowed my eyes, but took his phone and read the text he'd written.

In addendum to the above stated contractual text:

I rolled my eyes. "Using the big words, huh?"

Quincy shrugged.

*The undersigned agree that IF and WHEN an intimate, committed relationship proves successful, **Griffin Murphy-Sanders** will admit he was WRONG and should have listened to **Quincy Sanders** sooner.*

I scoffed. "Never."

"If you sign it, it's binding. Keep reading."

In addendum to the addendum:

IF and WHEN the above stated intimate and committed relationship reaches a milestone of both Griffin and Quincy graduating college, the mutually agreeing parties will entertain the prospect of making the relationship more permanent with a marriage proposal by one or the other of the undersigned.

I nearly gave myself whiplash jerking my head up to look at Quincy.

The asshole just grinned. "Come on, what's the risk? Admitting you were wrong? You're wrong all the time." He ran a foot along my leg. "And we're talking four years from now. No reason to look like a deer in the headlights. I just want it in there so we don't drag out *dating* forever."

I considered Quincy's additions. My part of the contract gave us both an out long before either of his addendums would go into effect. I was okay with it. I gave him a nod.

"Text that part to me. I'll add it to your part and sign." Quincy waited for the text to come through then did some copying and pasting before handing back my phone.

There, at the bottom of what we'd written, was his full name and the date.

I took a deep breath and added my own. "We'll print it and sign for real back at school."

"Agreed." He sat forward and held out a hand. "It's been a *pleasure* doing business with you, Mr. Murphy-Sanders."

Not for the first time in the recent past, electricity seemed to spark between our hands. I shook his hand, and he sat back with a grin.

We spent the next thirty minutes casting flirty glances toward each other, allowing our legs to touch more than what was strictly necessary, and having trouble hiding the ridiculous smiles on our faces.

* * *

LUNCH WAS a boisterous and loving affair. There was nothing I loved more than sitting down with Momma, Pops, and Quincy to eat delicious food and laugh. Would have been nice if Max had been there, but he was there in spirit.

By the time we'd eaten, helped clear the table, and finished washing and drying the dishes, the effects of the huge meal hit me. I yawned.

"You want to hit the road now or take a nap first?" Quincy asked as he caught my yawn.

"Nap, definitely. No way I could stay awake driving now."

"Agreed." Quincy hugged Momma and Pops. "Thank you for lunch. It was amazing as always. We're gonna sleep a couple hours before driving back."

"That sounds like a good idea." Momma kissed us both on the cheek.

Pops gave me a hug. "Nap? Uh-huh. I bet there's more than sleeping going on. I'll turn down my hearing-aid." He murmured to me and laughed.

My cheeks burst into flames.

Quincy and I headed up the stairs.

"What did Pops say to you?"

"Oh my God, he said he'd bet there'd be more than napping going on and he'd turn down his hearing aids." I flopped on the bed.

"I like the way Pops thinks." Quincy joined me on the bed.

Suddenly my heart was in my throat and I had no clue what to do with my arms or where to avert my gaze.

Quincy rolled to his side and placed a finger on my chin to turn my head toward him. "Grif, this doesn't have to be weird. It shouldn't be weird. If it *is*, we can stop."

I sighed. "I'm just nervous. What if I suck at…everything?"

"Well, sucking is definitely on the list of things I'd like to try." Quincy waggled his brow. "But let's just start slow. Come cuddle with me."

Quincy opened his arms and I moved quickly to lay my head on his chest. Being close to Quincy was as natural as breathing.

"What are you the most worried about?" Quincy's whispered against my head.

"I don't really know what I'm doing. I've kissed a couple guys, been kissed by a few, but that's it. I've given exactly one pretty blah blowjob. Couldn't stand for the guy to return the favor because I was shaking so bad and all I could think about was you. So, my *experience* includes giving a mediocre blowjob, a few kisses—one of those with *you*, a shit show with that David guy—which thankfully didn't turn into anything sexual, our mutual jackoff session, and waking up in your arms this morning." I buried my head into his chest. "How am I supposed to compete with what you've done?"

Quincy forced me to look at him again. "Just what experience do you assume I've had?"

I didn't want to think about him with other guys. "Aaron? And any other guys you've been with. That Jaylin guy you went out with a couple times?" I shrugged and my bottom lip pouted despite my attempts to act grown up.

Quincy chuckled. "Okay, truth time. Jaylin and I

kissed. He wanted more. I couldn't stop thinking about moving to college to be with you. Aaron and I kissed. He wanted more. I couldn't stop thinking about you in the next room. There's been a lot of kissing with quite a few guys. I've given a couple blowjobs and gotten a few in return." He leaned forward and kissed my cheek before whispering. "But nothing has ever gone farther than that. And that's all because of one reason." He nipped my earlobe. "Because my mind, heart, and body have been obsessed with one and only one person from the moment we first stroked each other right here in this bed so many years ago."

I shivered. "Yeah?"

He kissed my neck. "Absolutely."

As if my dormant inner sex fiend had just woken up, I arched my neck so Q could have better access. I groaned as his tongue teased.

"I only have one question," Quincy murmured.

"What?" I panted.

"Can I kiss you?" He palmed my cheek and brought our faces together.

The heat, sincerity, and anticipation in his eyes caused my breath to catch. I nodded and bit my lip.

Fire exploded in Q's eyes as he studied my lips. "I've wanted to kiss you for so long. Hold you in my arms. Call you mine." He caressed my cheek with his thumb. "This is so surreal, like a damn dream come true. I want to touch you, taste you, take you."

My cock throbbed at his words. "I want that, all of that. I want your lips, your mouth, your tongue, please." I groaned the moment Quincy thrust his cock against mine as he ran a thumb over my bottom lip.

He held my face in both hands as his mouth moved slowly to capture my lips.

Time stopped.

This was the moment I'd wanted for so long, but I'd been so afraid would ruin everything.

And it did.

Quincy's kiss ruined me for any other man. Ever.

The searing heat of his mouth, his tongue teasing my lips, caused me to gasp. Quincy took advantage of my open mouth and tentatively explored with his tongue.

I wrapped my arms around his neck and welcomed his tongue with abandon. Quincy shifted and moved his arms to hold me around the waist, never pausing as our tongues met, teased, and mated.

By the time we broke to breathe, I knew I'd never be the same. My heart soared in hopeful anticipation. But I also had the painful realization that I'd be crushed if Quincy ever wanted out of this. I'd respect it, of course, but how would I ever move on after the heat and perfection of that one kiss?

"You want to do more?" Quincy grumbled against my lips.

"More?"

"I want to strip you, lick, tease, and suck your entire body."

"Oh God," I groaned and pressed my cock against his. "I want that too."

"But?"

"It feels a little weird…"

Quincy jerked back. "No, baby. Please don't, not yet. Give it some time."

I chuckled. "*This* isn't weird." I rolled my hips again. "*This* is amazing. I'm just saying it's a little weird to take things much further with Momma and Pops right downstairs."

Quincy sighed and pressed his forehead against mine. "Oh my God. You scared me." He brought our lips together again and kissed me slowly. "Yeah, I hear ya. We'll stay fully clothed. For now. But once we're back at school, I'm tying you to my bed and not letting you go until we've done every damn sexy thing I've ever dreamed of doing to you."

I shuddered. "I'm in. *So* in. But we can definitely kiss for a bit longer. Then we *should* nap a little before the drive."

Quincy captured my lips again as our bodies writhed together. The pressure of his mouth against mine, the kisses on my neck, the roll of our hips, our cocks thrust together, were all too much.

I broke the kiss, panting. "Q, stop. I'm going to come in my pants."

He kissed me deeper. "Do it. Come for me."

"No, that would be so embarrassing."

"I'll come too. Do it. I'm close. We'll come together and be embarrassed together." He kissed me again, rocking his hips into mine. "But I won't be embarrassed because it's you, it's us, and there's nothing embarrassing about having my damn sexy-ass boyfriend in my arms and making him come."

I groaned and threw my head back, thrilling at Quincy's lips and tongue on my neck. Our cocks pressed against each other, both of us thrusting hard. "I'm close, oh God, so close."

Quincy's arms held me tight, his hips rolling against mine, and his lips at my ear. "Come for me, Grif. I want to see you lose control. Let go, baby."

My body tensed as my cock exploded warm stickiness. I moaned into Q's mouth as he kissed me through my orgasm. A moment later, Quincy paused and grunted against my lips as he found his own release.

A few moments later, my body completely sated, I groaned. "Grab that towel. This is going to get gross pretty soon."

Quincy moved off the bed to grab the towel. "Yeah, this was fine for now. But next time, no clothes. I need to see you come for me." He shifted his pants to wipe himself before crawling onto the bed and handing me the towel.

As I attempted to clean myself, Q whispered in my ear. "*Tonight*. Tonight, in my bed, I want you naked. I want your cock. I want your mouth. I want *all* of you."

Even as I wiped my cooling spunk from my boxers, my cock took an interest in Quincy's words. "Oh my God," I mumbled. "I've created a monster."

Quincy chuckled and palmed his junk. "I'll give you a monster."

"Oh my God, so cliché," I teased.

"Not interested?" Q challenged.

"I didn't say *that*." I jutted my chin as I tossed the towel to the floor.

Quincy kissed me and rolled us to our sides. "Sleep. We'll head back in a couple hours."

"I love you," I murmured before I even realized the words were coming. "I mean, I…"

Quincy's arms tightened. "It's okay, Grif. I've loved you since we were ten. Maybe a different kind of love then than now. But I get it. I love you, too." He kissed the side of my head. "So damn much."

I nodded into his chest. *So damn much* that my heart hurt. But it hurt in such an amazingly good way.

* * *

"THANK YOU, boys, for all of your help in the kitchen. This was looking to be a lonely Thanksgiving without having any fosters. Having you here made our entire holiday." Momma gushed as she followed us out the door.

When we stopped on the porch and dropped our bags in preparation for hugs, I simultaneously tensed and melted when Q took my hand.

Momma's laser sharp eyes took notice and took on a sparkly sheen. "How about you don't wait for a meddling old woman to tell you what's up next time, you hear? You boys are intelligent and quite capable of making good choices. But I won't turn down visits so I can meddle and sip the tea with you."

Quincy threw his head back in laughter. "Sip the tea? Have you been studying gay lingo in Urban Dictionary?"

Momma popped him on the head. "Maybe. A girl has to keep up." She wrapped us both in a hug and kissed our heads. "My boys, my *sons*, my greatest pride and joy. Momma is so proud of you."

"Greatest pride and joy, huh? I'm sure Dad will enjoy that one."

Momma harrumphed. "Max is amazing. You two are double that. Two for the price of one, a package deal of pride and joy."

Pops laughed and stepped up to hug us both.

Quincy let go of my hand long enough to give both Momma and Pops proper hugs.

I did the same.

Much love and hugs later, we picked up our bags and headed toward the car.

As soon as the bags were thrown in the trunk and we settled in the front, Quincy started the car, set a playlist on low volume, and put on his seatbelt before grabbing my hand again.

"Sorry, is this okay? I kinda feel like I've got a lot of hand holding to make up for."

I nodded. "I like it."

"No need to stop for food since I'm stuffed from lunch. Let me know if you need a bathroom break."

Quincy navigated the city streets until he hit the interstate.

About twenty minutes into the trip, after replaying the surreal events of the trip, anxiety began to creep in.

"What's up, G?" Quincy glanced my way. "I can feel tension in your hand. You having regrets?"

I chewed on my lip. "Not *regrets* exactly. Just questions and concerns."

"Spill. No secrets, no holding back. We talk this shit out. Always." He squeezed my hand.

"I guess I'm just wondering how all of this will work."

"The exact way it's been working since we were ten. I live with my best friend. I love my best friend. I support my best friend. But now, I also get to touch and hold and kiss my best friend."

"And sex?" I literally squeaked.

Q chuckled. "And sex." He winked. "Lots and lots of sex."

"But that's all just between us. I'm more concerned about the outside part."

Quincy frowned. "Tell me more."

"You're a sports management major. You're a student athlete. Do you really want to be saddled and stereotyped with a boyfriend who just does hair and makeup?" I worried my lower lip.

"Stop right there. Never again. Don't you dare put yourself down or think I'd be *saddled* with you." Quincy's nostrils flared. "First off, *I* wanted this as much or more than you. Second, how dare you downplay what you're doing? Do I want to be *saddled* with a boyfriend who is busting his ass as a business major *and* getting his cosmetology license? Damn straight, I do. You're the most talented, intelligent, and driven person I've ever known. When have I ever made you think I give a flying fuck about stereotypes or what people think?"

"I'm just saying that we're different. Sometimes different is difficult." I knew, deep down, that Quincy and I were soulmates. But I wanted him to have an out before my heart got any more involved than it already was.

"We've been different for almost a decade. Never stopped us from clicking. We may be different, but we *work*, Grif. Nothing has ever been as easy and as natural as being your friend. And taking that step toward *more* by kissing you? It was as easy as anything I've ever done. Different doesn't have to be difficult. In our case, different is just us. And it works." Quincy glanced my way. "So stop trying to offer me ways to back out of this." He squeezed my hand. "I love you. You love me. This is happening." He scowled. "Unless you're really wanting out of it?"

I shook my head, tears stinging my eyes. "No, I don't want out. I just want to make sure you know what you're getting into."

"I know. I accept. And I'm so damn excited for it." Quincy brought our clasped hands to his mouth and kissed my knuckles.

9

QUINCY

I TOOK Griffin's bag the moment we entered the suite and tossed both bags to the side before wrapping him in my arms.

Our faces nearly touched. I rubbed our noses together and let my lips hover over his.

"Hi. Welcome home." I nibbled at his ear.

Grif groaned and offered his neck for kisses. "I'm not sure how I lived this long without your lips on my neck."

"Never have to live in such horrid conditions again." I teased him as my lips trailed from his ear to his throat. "I want you in my bed, Grif. We don't have to do anything you're not comfortable with, but I want to touch you and hold you."

He groaned and nodded.

Once we reached my bedroom, I closed the door and flipped on the desk lamp. "Naked?"

Grif's hooded eyes met mine as he grabbed the hem of his shirt and pulled it over his head. His tongue shot out to lick his lips as he slowly shimmied out of his pants. His thick erection strained against the grey bikini briefs.

I palmed my cock and took a step toward Grif.

He smirked and nodded. "Naked."

I stripped in three seconds, loving the catch of Grif's breath when my dick smacked my stomach. I moved quickly and entered Grif's personal space. Our hard lengths rubbed together and I hooked my fingers in Grif's waistband. "This okay?"

He nodded and murmured, "Oh God, yes."

I pulled his underwear down his thighs and he stepped out of them. As if my hand and his cock were opposite poles of a magnet, I reached for his length and gripped. I ran my thumb through the droplet of liquid on his slit.

Griffin mirrored my actions and stroked my cock slowly. "We gonna jack each other like when we were sixteen?" His voice was thick with arousal.

"We could." I pumped his dick. "Or we could try something new."

"I'm game."

Grif shuddered when I dropped to my knees and the deep guttural moan he gave when I took him in my mouth was something I'd remember forever. I sucked and licked while I fondled his balls.

He jerked back with a gasp. "Wait, I don't want to go

first. Can I suck you? Then we can lay down and go from there?"

"God, Grif. You can suck me any damn time you want."

He spun me around and pushed me to the bed. The vision of Griffin kneeling between my spread thighs, his eyes intent on my cock, was something I'd treasure forever. "I'm sorry if I'm not good at this..." he began, but I cut him off.

"If my cock is in your mouth, it will be amazing. Period."

Grif's perfect pink lips parted, and I sank my dick slowly into his hot mouth. I leaned back on my arms with a loud groan. I'd died and gone to heaven. "Get on the bed." I moved so that I was flat on my back. "Straddle my chest and suck me."

Grif's cheeks pinked, but he followed my directions and positioned himself onto my chest, his ass at my face before he bent to suck me. As the heat of his mouth engulfed my cock again, I rolled us to the side to suck his length deep, my nose bumping his balls.

Griffin faltered momentarily in his movements but recovered quickly.

When I popped off his dick and shifted to tongue his asshole, Griffin's arms gave out and he fell to his elbows. "Oh God, Q. What the fuck? God that's good."

I hummed and rimmed him again.

"I want to try that." Grif mumbled before swallowing my cock again.

"Soon. But this is all me today." I slicked a finger in

my mouth and teased his hole slowly until he opened for me. "I want you to come down my throat while I finger your ass, G."

He whimpered and sucked me harder as I continued to finger him and take him deep in my mouth.

All too soon, our bodies gave in to the pleasure and we both erupted. His warmth was salty and bitter on my tongue as I swallowed all he gave me.

Griffin groaned around my cock as I shot down his throat.

When we caught our breaths and came back to earth, I grabbed a washcloth from the bathroom and cleaned myself up before tossing it to him.

"I know you've probably got studying to do a lot of nights, but I'd love to have you in here with me whenever possible." I rolled him into my arms and kissed him deeply, the flavor of our releases still clinging to our lips.

"Mmm, I can make that happen." Griffin mumbled against my lips. "Do you think you'll want anal sex? I'm interested, but it's okay if you're not. I know not everyone is."

I growled against his ear. "I'm very interested. I think I'd mostly like to top, but I know the very first time we do that I'd like you to top me."

Grif drew back with shock in his eyes. "What? Why?"

I shrugged. "I've always imagined taking your ass, but the first time needs to be you taking me. If you're okay with that, I mean. I *want* your cock in me almost as much as I want to fuck you. I just need to know we're okay with anal and, in my mind, that means me bottoming first."

Griffin was quiet for a moment. "That's okay. I've always imagined you topping me. Oh God," he groaned. "You have *no* idea how much I've imagined that."

I laughed. "Yeah, pretty sure I know how much because I've been doing the same."

"I'll gladly top you, but I think I'm going to like it the other way around mostly."

I nodded. "That's okay. I just feel like it needs to be me taking it first."

"Any idea of when this might happen?" Griffin whispered.

"Whenever it feels right." I kissed him.

"I'm down with that." He sighed against my chest. "Q?"

"Yeah?"

"This was really good. *Really* good. And I love you." His voice was sleepy.

"Totally agree. So good. And I love you, G."

Pops died a week after Thanksgiving.

Dad called me late one night. "Momma just called to let me know Pops died in his sleep. He was sleeping in his recliner and didn't come for dinner when she called. She thought he'd turned off his hearing aid."

"Oh my God." Tears stung my eyes. Pops had been

as much, if not more, a father to me as my own dad. "Is she okay?"

"She is. She's sad, but she and Pops had something very special. She's grateful he didn't suffer. She holds fast to knowing they'll be together again."

"When is the funeral?"

"No funeral. Pops didn't want one. Momma is having him cremated and taking him down to Florida. She'll stay with her sister until at least spring."

"Oh, wow. Okay. We should go see her." I wiped tears from my cheeks.

"She told me she'd call you and Griffin tomorrow. She estimates three to five days to take care of Pops' affairs, pack, receive his ashes, and hit the road to Florida. She said she was going to be busy and didn't want you to miss classes; I think she needs some time to process and heal. Being with her sister will be good for her." Dad must have been up late working. I heard a keyboard in the background. "She did indicate that you guys should come visit in the winter to get away from the cold."

"Yeah, we'll do that." I agreed absently. My heart ached at the thought of Pops being gone. But his voice echoed in my mind; I knew he'd tell me to remember him with love and *keep on keeping on*. That was just the type of man Pops was.

"Speaking of *you guys*. Momma said you and Griffin are dating?"

I smiled despite that sadness in my heart. "Yeah, we are. It's something we've both wanted but been worried would mess up our friendship. But we decided to take the risk. Didn't want to be forty and regret that we never took the leap and let love happen."

"Well, congratulations. You two have always had something special. I'm very happy for you."

Dad and I spoke for a few more minutes before hanging up.

I checked the time. Griffin had said earlier that he was going to his room to study. We'd spent every night in my bed, but he retreated to his room when he needed to concentrate on school work.

I sighed. I hated to interrupt. And I knew this would shake him. But I couldn't *not* tell him Pops had passed away.

I crossed through the bathroom to his room.

Griffin looked up and smiled. "Hey, give me a few minutes and I'll be finished." His smile faded. "What's wrong?"

"Pops died."

Griffin's face fell, tears filling his eyes. "Oh no, what happened?"

I went to his bed and moved his books aside before climbing in beside him. "Dad just called. Momma had called him. Said Pops died in his sleep."

Griffin sniffed and wiped his nose. "Funeral?"

"No." I shook my head. "Pops didn't want any of that. Momma's having him cremated and she's taking his ashes to Florida. She's going to stay with her sister at least until Spring. She wants us to come down over winter break."

He shuddered in my arms. "I'm so sorry for crying. I should be comforting you."

"Why should you be sorry for crying?" I wiped my own eyes. "He was your family. He was your adopted *father*. You have every right to be sad."

"He was your biological grandfather and raised you as much as your own dad did."

"It's not a competition, G. We can both be sad." I hugged him tighter.

"That's just like Pops to not want a funeral or anything fancy." Griffin chuckled.

"Right? I was thinking the same thing."

"I feel bad for Momma though. Feels like we should do more."

I nodded. "I said the same thing, but Dad thinks she needs some time to process and heal. He said Momma wants us to know she'll call us in a few days." I smiled sadly. "Momma and Pops had a special relationship. She'll miss him, but I think being in Florida with her sister will be good. Want to plan a trip down there over break?"

Griffin wiped his eyes again. "Definitely. And we should send her flowers or something. Oh! How about a bouquet-a-month type thing once she's settled?"

"Perfect. We'll start it next week." My heart was both achy and full with sadness over losing Pops and love for Griffin and his enormous heart.

Griffin nodded. "Movie?"

"It's late. No early classes?"

"A couple hours won't hurt. Classes aren't until ten

tomorrow." Griffin sniffled one last time. "Pick something."

I nodded and rummaged through Griffin's collection. "*Lilo and Stitch?*"

Griffin's watery smile warmed my heart. "Perfect."

We climbed into Griffin's bed and cuddled under the blanket.

By the time the credits rolled, I couldn't help the smile on my face.

"What are you smiling about?" Griffin asked.

"Just that you're starting to rub off on me, and I'm finding deeper meanings in all these movies you love so much." I shrugged and kissed the top of his head.

"Oh yeah, like what?" Griffin challenged.

"First, it made me think of you. All of your makeup and dancing and movies. I love that you're different, I love that you're doing what you love. The movie shows that the people who matter will accept you no matter what. And I feel that deep down." I brushed a kiss across his lips. "Second, maybe most important, is the *Ohana means family* theme. You became part of our family from the moment Momma brought you into my room. Blood isn't what makes a family; bonds make a family. *Ohana*. It's the family we're born with and also the family we make. You, me, Momma, Pops, Dad, we're family. The bond you and I have is stronger than any blood relation."

Griffin kissed me softly. "And thank God for that. Sex with my actual blood-related brother would be frowned upon. Although, honestly, I say *down with kink shaming*."

I snorted. "Truth."

He lunged for me and deepened the kiss, his tongue slipping between my lips as he moaned into my mouth. "I'm so ready to have sexy time with you. But it's going to have to wait. It's after midnight and we both need sleep."

I nodded and pulled him into my arms. "Sleep, baby. I have an early alarm set on my phone."

"I'm going to miss Pops." Grif shuddered in my arms.

"I know. Me too." I kissed the top of his head. "I'm glad he got to see us together before he left us."

"Same."

* * *

"So, the bad news is that Dad is going overseas for a while and won't be home for Christmas." I hung up the phone as I entered the living room where Griffin and I were putting up our first *together* Christmas tree.

Grif made a pouty face. "Tell me there's some good news."

I put my arms around his waist and pulled his back to my front while kissing his neck. "We get to spend our first Christmas together right here making memories and traditions."

"That sounds fun." Grif worried his lip.

"But?"

He shrugged. "I want to do gifts, but I don't have a ton of money. So, we have to do cheap or no cost gifts, okay?"

"Just being here with you is all I need, but okay."

"Should we do a whole holiday meal?" Grif's face was hopeful.

"I think we should at least attempt it." I turned him to face me and hugged him close. "And have the sushi menu ready just in case."

He laughed. "Good plan."

* * *

"MERRY CHRISTMAS," I whispered in Griffin's ear on Christmas morning. "I say we pop those cinnamon rolls in the oven and pray we didn't fuck up Momma's recipe too bad. Then we open presents."

"Mmmm," Grif mumbled. "What time is it?"

"Five?"

"Too early, Q. More sleep." He rolled over and snuggled deep into the blankets.

I kissed him. "Okay. I'm going to fix the cinnamon rolls and prep the tea and coffee. You should come join me within an hour or I may open all the gifts."

"We said no pricey gifts," Griffin protested.

"I didn't do anything pricey. Not at all. But Momma and Dad sent gifts and I *really* want to open them."

"Okay, let me sleep a few more minutes."

I slapped his ass as I rolled from the bed.

Twenty minutes later, the cinnamon rolls were

smelling heavenly and I was sipping coffee while Grif's water heated for tea.

He came shuffling into the kitchen. "You don't play fair. Those smell so good." Grif took a deep breath and moaned. "Oh my God, that smells just like every Christmas morning at Momma and Pops' place." He gave me a watery smile and I knew he was thinking about Momma and Pops just as much as I was.

"We'll have to tell her that her recipe worked out perfectly when we get to Florida."

"Let's not get ahead of ourselves. We need to *taste* them first." Griffin bumped my hip with his.

"True. But they smell just the same."

And the rolls did turn out amazing. I was proud of how well we'd done.

"Now if only lunch can turn out just as well." Grif smiled over a large bite of cinnamon roll.

"Let's get the chicken and veggies in the oven to bake slowly while we open gifts and shower." I finished my cinnamon roll and took my plate to the sink before sliding the baking dish into the oven. "I'll cover the rolls for later."

Grif finished his breakfast and began to wash the dishes. I loved how we fell into such a natural routine when we were together.

"Okay, presents!" I crowed when the last plate and mug were dried and put away.

"You haven't changed a bit." Griffin wrapped his arms around my neck. "You were always so excited and loud on Christmas morning."

I kissed him, but frowned as memories washed over me. "And you always seemed to get quieter and sadder on Christmas."

He shrugged. "Makes me miss my mom. She always tried to make Christmas nice. My father usually ruined it, but she always tried. And no matter how much I knew you all wanted me and accepted me and loved me, I usually had this voice in the back of my head telling me that I didn't belong. That I'd never really belong anywhere."

I took Grif's face in my hands and made him look at me. "Stop. Never again. You *always* belonged. You *do* belong. You *will* *always* belong. With me. Forever. Momma and Pops were as proud to call you their own as they were to call me their own." I kissed him softly and whispered, "Always and forever," against his mouth.

We sorted through the presents Momma and Dad had sent. When the two piles were on the couch, we settled in next to each other.

"Take turns?" I asked. "Rock, paper, scissors to see who starts?"

"Always so competitive," Grif teased. "You can start because we both know you'll pout if you don't get to go first."

I started to argue, but I was too excited. I tore into my first gift. A top-of-the-line stop watch I could use in several different ways in my degree.

Griffin gasped as he opened a collection of makeup

brushes. "Oh my God, these are *so nice*." He ran a hand over them reverently.

I knew the items Momma and my dad had gotten for Grif. He was likely to be in tears by the end of opening presents.

My next present was a sweet new suit. I didn't have many opportunities to dress up, but the suit would be perfect when I had sports awards and future meetings and drafts for clients.

Grif tore into another package. "No way," he breathed as he opened a flat iron.

I knew nothing of his hair and makeup tools, but he'd always said this one was top-notch.

"This is too much," Griffin protested with a shake of his head.

"Nah, you know Momma and Max love to give gifts. They can afford it. If they couldn't, they wouldn't." I kissed his cheek. "You deserve the best."

I chuckled at the coffee cup I opened next. *It's a sports management thing, you wouldn't understand* was printed on the mug.

"You've got to be shitting me." Griffin's eyes were wide as he pulled a blow dryer from the next package. "This is like the exact one I've been lusting over." He shot me a look. "Did you tell them what to buy?"

I shrugged. "Maybe. Momma wanted to get the things you really wanted." I moved on to my last gift. "Sweet!" I waved tickets in the air. "Season tickets for basketball *and* football."

Grif's last gift set the tears in motion. "Holy shit." He hugged the shears to his chest. "They are gorgeous!" His words were shaky and the tears sparkled on his cheeks.

"You love them?" I smiled.

He nodded. "But it's all too much."

"Well, you can't return them. You know Momma doesn't give receipts unless you can prove you're getting something just as nice when you return the gift." I thumbed a tear from Grif's cheek.

"What's that smell?" Griff sniffed the air.

"Probably lunch."

"It smells like smoke." Griff stood and headed toward the kitchen. When he yanked the oven open, smoke poured out. "Shit, open the windows. We're going to set off the smoke detectors." He flipped the oven knobs to *off* and donned oven mitts to pull out the smoking baking dish.

I opened the windows, pointed the fans to blow the smoke out of the suite, and grabbed a chair to stand on in case I needed to turn off the smoke detector.

Griffin pulled back the foil on the baking dish. "Shit, everything is charred."

I left the chair and went to look over his shoulder. "Fuck, I thought I followed the directions just right."

"Wasn't there supposed to be some sort of sauce or liquid?" Grif poked the burned veggies with a fork. "And you turned the oven down, right?"

I winced. "Liquid. I forgot the liquid. I was going to add it this morning; I was afraid it would get mushy overnight."

"And the oven temperature?"

Through a grimace, I mumbled, "I think I forgot to turn the oven down after the cinnamon rolls."

Griffin sighed. "Yeah, I think it was supposed to go a lot lower so the meat and veggies could cook slowly."

"I'm sorry. The cinnamon rolls were so good, I may have gotten a little cocky and not followed all the directions." I truly did feel bad.

Grif smiled and hugged me. "No worries. We can try to be big boys and cook the chicken and veggies another time."

"But what about lunch?" I mumbled into his neck.

"Well, we've got delicious cinnamon rolls to tide us over." Grif kissed the corner of my mouth. "I bet there are some sushi places open. You know I'm always game for sushi."

I captured his mouth in a kiss. "Sorry I messed up lunch, but sushi does sound good."

"Nothing is messed up because we're together," Grif whispered against my lips. "And we still have our gifts from each other to open."

LUCKILY, we found a sushi restaurant open. Actually, quite a few places were open. It was a reminder that not *all* in the town or our country celebrated Christmas. Also, I assumed that many restaurants figured they'd get plenty of college students in for food. Maybe not all students burned their first attempt at a lunch that didn't include take-out or frozen pizza, but I'm sure many weren't cooking either way.

"Honestly," Griffin began after the host seated us, "as good as I'm sure the chicken and veggies could have been, a Dragon Ball sounds just as amazing."

"Truth. So, four Dragon Balls? What else?" I glanced at the menu. "Tiger Roll?"

"Yes, and a California Roll, of course." Griffin sipped his water and pushed his menu to the side.

I gave the server our order and scooted closer to Griffin in our private, round corner booth. The restaurant was one of our favorites because it was quiet and friendly and had the best rolls and prices.

"This is nice. Maybe we make this our Christmas Day tradition." I took Grif's hand.

"Save the smoke detectors?" he teased.

"I'm really surprised we didn't set them off."

"I think a few more minutes would have caused a lot more damage. You were quick with the fans. How embarrassing would it have been if the whole building had to evacuate because we can't cook some Christmas chicken?"

We both laughed.

An older woman bustled to our table with our food. Griffin started to move his hand from mine, but I kept his tight in mine. The server placed our tray of food at the edge of the table and smiled brightly. She reached over and laid her hand on top of our joined ones. "A very happy day to you." She then pointed to our tray and named the rolls despite the fact we'd eaten here so many times we didn't need a reminder.

"That was sweet." Griffin nodded toward her retreating back. "But I need my hand to devour this food." He bumped his shoulder against mine. "You can have it back later."

"Fine." I pretended to pout. "But I want more than your hand later."

"Gifts later, right?" Grif raised his brows.

"Gifts later. But *later* later it's sexy time," I growled against his ear and grinned evilly when Griffin shrugged.

We talked about Pops and Momma, our new gifts, what we needed to pack for the trip to see Momma in Florida, and the new classes that would start after break while we ate.

When the bill came, Grif and I both reached for it at the same time. "I've got it," I said.

"Why? Because I'm the poor boy?" Griffin scowled.

"What? No, just my treat."

"So, we used to split things, but now I'm your kept boyfriend?"

"Whoa, what the hell, G? I've treated before. You've treated before. Since I'm pretty much responsible for burning our lunch, I figured it was only right for me to treat today." I patted his leg. "You may be my boyfriend, but you're not *kept* by anyone."

He winced. "Sorry, money is such a touchy subject for me. Especially since I don't have much of it. But I never want to appear like I'm taking advantage of your money."

"Don't even worry about it. Consider it part of your Christmas gift."

"No! We said no money on gifts." Griffin's eyes pleaded with mine.

"Fine, fine. Just lunch, not a gift." I knew Grif was sensitive about money. He had been since the very first day he was placed at Momma and Pops' house. Always balked at new clothes or toys or gifts. Always tried to order the cheapest item from the menu. Always trying to do extra chores around the house as if Momma expected him to earn his keep.

I paid the bill and left a generous tip before Grif and I headed toward the car.

"Anywhere else you want to go before we go back home?" I started the car and pulled from the parking lot.

"No, just home. I'm ready to give you your gift."

"You're my gift." It sounded cheesy, but I meant it.

Grif snorted and rolled his eyes. "That's sweet. You're mine, too. And *me* is about all you're getting."

"Anything you give me is perfect. I hope you like what I'm giving you."

"Is that an innuendo?" Griffin smirked. "Because I've really liked what you've *given* me so far."

"Oh, I'm giving you something, but no, your gift isn't just sex."

Once we got home, we made hot chocolate and sat

on the couch. I handed G an envelope and he laughed as he handed me one as well.

"We're both such amazing wrappers." Grif bit his lip.

"Open at the same time?" I waved the envelope in the air.

Griffin nodded and we both tore into our gifts.

Griffin cooed and launched himself at me. "A double-feature of any two movies of my choice *and* I get to do your makeup? Awwww, you really do love me."

I kissed him deeply, loving the feel of his body stretched out on top of mine. "You know I do. And this? Just making out on the couch could be your gift to me and I'd love it."

"Nope, read yours. Sorry, I tackled you before you got to."

I pulled the paper from the envelope and read it aloud, "Two hours of video gaming *of Quincy's choice* and a dance." I smiled and glanced at him. "A dance?"

Grif shrugged. "I was thinking like a sexy dance, just for you. I may have new underwear for the occasion."

I wrapped my arms around him and pulled him to lay on top of me again. "You weren't supposed to buy anything," I reminded him as I kissed my way along his jaw until I reached his lips for a kiss.

He shrugged. "A guy needs underwear. My need for underwear just coincided with a lap dance I want to give to you."

I groaned. "I can't wait." Griffin was an amazing dancer. I loved to watch him lose himself in the music.

But sexy underwear and a dance just for me? It would be perfection.

An hour later, Griffin had transformed my face into a work of art. I wasn't even kidding, what that man could do with makeup and brushes was a true talent. "Babe, if you wanted to do my makeup every day, I'd seriously consider wearing this on the daily. I'm hot as shit."

Grif laughed and wrapped his arms around me.

I pulled away. "No, no messing up my face."

"Okay, well no daily makeup for you if I can't even kiss you."

"Babe, I can't let you mess with this perfection."

Grif rolled his eyes. "I want to pick two movies you've never seen." He came back with ten DVDs. "Which ones have you not seen?"

I pulled the four I'd never seen, plus *Winnie the Pooh* despite having seen it before.

Grif raised a brow.

"What? I like this one." I smiled and shrugged.

He huffed and shook his head. "I just don't even know how you've been my best friend for so long and not watched every single Disney movie." Griffin picked *Mulan* and *The Many Adventures of Winnie the Pooh*. "We'll do these today. I know you've watched *Pooh*, but it's such a good one."

Nearly three hours later, Grif sighed as the credits rolled. "I love those movies."

"You love almost all Disney movies."

"True." He smiled and kissed me. "Did you like them?"

"I did. I think being around you and watching these movies with you has forced me to look deeper into them."

"Yeah? What did you get from the two today?"

"Well, I know you've told me this one before, but I think I get it a little more now. *The Many Adventures of Winnie the Pooh* teaches that close friends are life's greatest and most abiding treasures; cherish your time together. And I very much cherish all the time we've had together. I look forward to a lot more time with you." I kissed his neck. "I liked the quote, *'If there ever comes a day when we can't be together, keep me in your heart. I'll stay there forever.'* I never want to think about us not being together, but if it comes to that, I feel like we'd stay forever in each other's hearts."

Grif wiped his eyes. "Oh my God, that's the sweetest thing ever." He kissed me. "What about *Mulan*?"

"I felt *Mulan* was very good. Not better or worse than *Winnie the Pooh*, just different. I think the lesson is be strong, be independent. But most importantly, be yourself, no matter what other people think. And that is so very perfect for you, for me, and for *us*. The quote I liked best was the one about *'The flower that blooms in adversity is the most rare and beautiful of all.'* You are the perfect example of that quote. You've overcome so much despite the shit handed to you. And you've come out on the other side of it strong, independent, and successful."

"I'm not sure I'd say independent or successful just yet." Grif wrinkled his nose.

"You are. And you'll gain more independence and success with each passing day." I wrapped him in my arms. "Just don't get so independent and successful that you don't need or want me around."

"Never," Grif mumbled into my neck. "Video game time?"

"Yes, because once you dance for me, I'm taking you to bed for the rest of the night." I ran a hand from his shoulder down to his ass and squeezed. "Any choice of video game?"

"Nope, it's your gift so you get to choose."

I picked *Marvel Ultimate Alliance,* and we settled in for an amazing two hours of laughing, teasing, smack-talking, and arguing. By the time we reached the end of our time, my eyes desperately needed a break from the screen. "We should do this more often. All of it. Makeup, movies, video games."

"Truth."

"And sexy dancing that leads to you in my bed." I waggled my brows. "I'm ready for my dance."

Grif blushed. "Okay. Sit on the couch. I'm going to change my clothes."

I was equal parts nervous and turned on as I waited for Grif to come back. Bottoming had never really been something I'd wanted to do. Except for Griffin. I'd never really been interested in topping anyone. Except for Griffin. Making out and some blow jobs with others were fine, but every single kiss, every blow job, ended with me thinking about one thing. Griffin.

And now I sat on our couch, in our suite, waiting for Griffin, *my boyfriend*, to put on underwear he bought specifically for me and to dance for me. Never let anyone say that dreams don't come true.

Griffin cleared his throat from behind me and I turned to see him leaned against his bedroom door wrapped in a black silk robe. He looked as nervous as I felt, but the way he bit his lip let me know he was also just as turned on as me.

He sauntered to the kitchen and turned off the light before he dimmed the two living room lamps. Grif slid his phone from the robe pocket and messed with it before Rihanna's "Skin" filled the room. The transition was instantaneous; Grif's eyes were dark and sultry as he drifted across the room in rhythm to the song.

Once Griffin stood in front of me, his back to me, the robe slipping from one shoulder, I noticed he was wearing fucking black heels, and I nearly busted a nut right there on the couch.

The robe slipped from the other shoulder, and Griffin rolled his hips as he turned around. He used the black silk as a sexy-as-fuck prop as he slid the material against his skin, teased flashes of skin underneath, and twisted the fabric in his hands. I wanted to grab him, tear the robe from his body, and kiss him from head to toe, but I couldn't move, couldn't take my eyes off him.

He strutted slowly away from me, spread his legs, and bent over to wrap long, graceful fingers around his ankles. The robe rode up and taunted me with a tiny peek at the curves of his ass cheeks in what appeared to be a Y-Back black mesh thong. Holy hell.

Griffin teased the robe up higher on his ass and gave his ass a shake before he smacked a perfectly round cheek with his hand and gave it a squeeze.

"Fuuuck," I moaned and adjusted my hard length.

He twirled around and gave me a wicked grin before gliding toward me. Just when I thought he was going to touch me, Griffin stopped and dropped into a squat. Robe gathered around his waist, elbows on his knees, and one thumb tracing his bottom lip.

My heart pounded in my chest, and I had to put my hands under my legs to control the desire I had to pull him to me. He was so very close, but still too far away. Griffin smirked at my hands under my legs. Sexy fucker knew he had me fucked up.

Grif stood and popped his right hip, heeled left foot turned out as he trailed a hand up his thigh and cupped his cock before hooded eyes met mine. He swiveled his hips in small circles as he turned his back to me again. Glancing over his shoulder, he shimmied the robe in hella slow increments from his elbows down to his waist, over his hips, and finally let it fall to the floor in a billowy mass of black silk. His pale skin was still pink where he'd smacked his own ass and he rubbed a hand over it slowly. The strips of black material stretched across his ass and contrasted beautifully with his skin. When he finally swung his hips around to face me, he dipped his thumbs into the waistband and teased the mesh-front thong down his hips slightly. His plump cock filled the material and I nearly bit through my tongue wanting to touch him.

Griffin's movements matched the rhythm of the song and never once faltered as he moved across the last few feet between us to pull me to the edge of the cushion before he straddled my lap. He stripped my shirt over my head and then pushed me to lean back on the couch.

My hands reached for him but he shook his head and moved my arms to rest behind my head before he trailed his hands down my chest. He teased my nipples, ran a finger down the middle of my abs, and dipped his fingers under my waistband for a brief moment.

He shifted from straddling my lap to my hips so his ass could grind against my cock. Hands running through his own hair, hips gyrating, Griffin looked down at me and teased his tongue along his lips.

"Jesus," I huffed out. "You're gonna kill me, G."

He smirked and ran his hands from my bent elbows to my hands and then moved my hands to his hips as he continued to rock himself on my cock.

I skimmed my hands from his hips to his ass and squeezed his cheeks hard before teasing a finger along his exposed crack. Griffin shuddered and leaned forward to kiss me. All control I had pretended to have flew out the window and I wrapped my arms around him and stood from the couch. Rihanna reached the end of her lyrics, but he must have put it on repeat because she started in on "Skin" again as I reached the doorway to my bedroom. I'd never hear the song for the rest of my life without thinking about Griffin dancing for me and our first time having sex.

I dropped Grif on my bed and skimmed my hands from one thigh to his foot to remove the black patent-leather heel before repeating the movement on the other thigh before removing the second shoe. His long legs hung over the edge of my bed, and I stood between his legs and hooked my fingers under his waistband before leaning over to press kisses against his inner thighs and tongue his cock through the black mesh.

"You like the underwear?" Griffin propped himself up on his elbows and watched as I mouthed his dick.

"Best underwear I've ever seen in my entire life." I whispered my words against his lower belly before licking the thin trail of hair up to his bellybutton. "But now I need to see them off of you." I pulled gently on the elastic and moved the material slowly down Grif's thighs until he was completely naked.

"I feel a little underdressed." Grif kept his eyes on me as he gripped his cock.

I stepped away and paused with my hands on my fly. I'd never be as graceful as Griffin, but I allowed the rhythm of the song to set my movements. With a little hip action of my own, I turned around and teased my jeans from my waist, over the swell of my ass, and past my thighs until the pants were at my ankles and I kicked them toward the wall. I began again with my boxer briefs, swiveling my hips, shimmying the material down slowly until I was completely naked.

"Oh my God."

I heard G's low groan and turned toward him with a wink. "Like what you see?" My heart thudded and my breath caught as I took in Grif's body spread out before me, his cock fully erect, and his eyes appraising me from head to toe.

Grif nodded slowly and licked his lips.

I crawled between his legs and gathered him in my arms before capturing his mouth in a kiss that blended perfectly with the rhythm of the music filling the suite. Our tongues danced, tasted, teased, and thrust. "You want to stop with this? We could have plenty of fun just like this." *I* didn't want to stop. Not at all. But I didn't want Griffin to feel pressured. That was part of why I wanted to bottom this first time.

Grif shook his head and palmed my cheek. "I'm so fucking nervous, but I don't want to stop."

Turning my head, I pressed a kiss against his palm. "Tell me what you're nervous about."

He took a deep breath. "Doing it wrong, hurting you, sucking at it."

I chuckled. "Insert Tab A into Slot B. Easy peasy."

Grif snorted.

"Baby, I've dreamed of sex with you basically since I figured out what sex was. I'm anxious about it, but it's a good anxious. I want this with you. I want to give you this." I wrapped a hand around his neck and pulled him in for a kiss. "Now, I'm dying to get your cock in my ass if you're ready."

"Sweet talker," Grif teased. "I'm nervous, but I'm ready. You have condoms and lube, right?"

I rolled to the side and fumbled with the side table drawer until I reached the foil packets and bottle I was searching for. I held them up with a waggle of my brows.

"Did you, um, do any *other* type of preparation?" He grimaced. "I mean, I'm not completely familiar with all of that, but um," he babbled.

I huffed a laugh. "Taken care of. That was an experience."

When Grif's eyes widened, I stopped him.

"Not in a terrible way. Just new. But the pathway has been cleared for your journey."

Grif groaned. "Oh my God, I need you to never say that again. And later you need to give me the pertinent details so I can do the same." He was cute when he rambled nervously.

"Get. In. My. Ass." I muscled the two of us to lay parallel with the bed and pulled him on top of me. Grif fit perfectly between my spread legs and our heavy cocks took a renewed interest in the conversation as they met and rubbed together.

"How do you want to be? On your back? Your knees? On top?" Grif worried his lip.

"Just like this. On my back, you between my legs. I want to see your face. I want you controlling everything." My breath hitched on the words. "Do you want to prep me or want me to do it?"

"As appealing as the thought of watching you finger

yourself is," Grif smirked, "if I'm going to control everything, I think I'd like to do it." He grabbed the lube and snapped the lid open. First time nerves must have gotten the best of him because he dumped about a gallon of liquid into his palm. "Shit, that's a bit of an overkill." He winced.

I laughed. "No worries, baby. We'll have to wash the sheets anyway."

Grif laid to my side, his head aligned with my bellybutton, and slowly trailed his slick fingers toward my ass. My cock jerked as he teased my taint. My legs fell open more as Grif probed at my hole.

"This okay?" Grif's face was a mix of terror, lust, and concern.

"Do it. Press it in."

I couldn't help the gasp as his finger breached me. It stung.

"Sorry." He paused.

"Don't. Move it. Add another. It's kinda stingy but it's not painful."

Grif spent the next few minutes stretching me, finger fucking me, and studying my face to be sure I was okay. Worrying about me, protecting me as a lover just as he always had as a friend and brother.

"I'm ready, G. I want more. I want your cock." I gripped my own dick and squeezed hard.

Griffin fumbled to open the condom with his extra slick hands, but he finally ripped it open with his teeth and rolled it down his hard length. Slicking his cock first, Grif reached for a pillow. "Put this under your hips. I think it will give a better angle."

I doubled the pillow and slid it under my ass to prop myself up.

"Please don't let this hurt or suck," Grif mumbled in sort of a soft prayer.

I laughed. "I want it, G. Now."

The first press of his cock against my hole set me on fire. As he slid in slowly, inch by inch, that fire grew. The sensations overwhelmed me. The stretch, the sting, the fullness all mixed with the heat of Grif's cock, the fever of his skin against mine, and the look of total bliss on his face as he sank deeper into my ass. We were one, united, and it felt like my entire world was complete.

"Holy fuck," Griffin gritted out between clenched teeth. "You're so fucking tight."

"Move, G. Fuck me." My cock had softened a bit with the initial discomfort, but I gripped it and stroked.

Grif began to pump his hips in an unsure rhythm. "Are you okay?"

"Yeah, baby. I'm amazing. You can go slow or fast, whatever feels right. Just fucking move."

He finally settled into a smooth, slow rhythm, and I threw my head back in pleasure. It felt so fucking good.

Griffin moaned. "Q, I'm not going to be able to do this for long. I'm going to come."

"Watch me jack myself as you fuck me. I'm not far behind you." I continued stroking my cock as his thrusts increased in speed and power. When he hit me deep, I saw stars and my balls drew up tight. "Shit, G. Do that again."

He thrust deep and hard several more times before he paused with his cock buried in my ass and groaned. His dick throbbed deep in my body as he unloaded his release.

With a final stroke of my cock, I painted my chest with a roar.

Griffin collapsed on top of me, smearing my cum between us.

"Holy fucking shit," he growled. "That was beyond amazing. I'm so glad I never did that with anyone before you."

"Same." And then I thought about what he said. "Baby, I can't even breathe thinking about you doing that with someone else. Or me even trying to find pleasure like that with someone else."

"No worries, Q. I don't know that I could *ever* be relaxed enough with someone else to do that with them. You're the only person I ever want to be this close to." He groaned a little and pulled from my body slowly. "You want to shower?"

"Yeah." I winced at the feeling of emptiness. "We better wash these sheets."

Griffin gathered the lube splattered sheets. "I'll toss them in the washer. You get the shower started."

He met me in the bathroom a few moments later. I stepped into the shower and held my hand out for him. We rinsed and then I wrapped him in my arms. "That was fucking amazing. I love you so damn much."

Grif shuddered in my arms. "It was so good." He chuckled. "Never really thought about topping. And I definitely want to bottom too. But watching your body under me, open for me, responding to my touch, coming apart because of me, *with* me? So fucking good."

We kissed soft and slow until the water began to run cold. Quickly soaping our bodies and shampooing our hair, we finished in cold water.

"Double showers with making out should maybe *start* with washing next time." I tossed a towel at Griffin.

He dried himself but I caught his gaze stop at the box on the counter.

"You want me to tell you about it? Or figure it out for yourself?" I nodded toward the package. I'd felt silly buying the economy pack of douches, but I figured we'd use them plenty. At least until we figure all the sex stuff out and settled into knowing our bodies' needs and what we liked.

"Um," Grif blushed. "I've been reading. I think I can figure it out. Keep a little mystery between us so as to not kill the romance, huh?"

I laughed. "Sounds good." I kissed him. "But promise, it didn't hurt. Wasn't difficult."

"Good to know." Grif chewed on his bottom lip. "My turn tomorrow, yeah?"

"Only if that's what you want." I pulled him close.

"Oh, I want. Definitely." He nodded and smiled. "Morning sex and then we head to see Momma."

"Sounds like the perfect plan." I nibbled at his ear and kissed along his neck. "Sleep in your bed tonight?"

We spent a couple hours talking and checking social media before I couldn't keep my eyes open. I hugged Grif to my chest. "I love you. Merry Christmas, G."

He kissed my chin. "Love you more."

We drifted to sleep in each other's arms.

* * *

GRIF MOVED and the bed shifted early the next morning before he rolled from bed and padded to the bathroom. In my sleepy haze, I heard the shower, but I slipped back into my sleep coma without giving it a second thought.

Later, I wasn't sure how much later, but the sun was up, Grif climbed back into bed. "Hey, I switched the sheets to the dryer since we forgot last night." He kissed me.

"No fair, you've showered and brushed your teeth?" The scent of soap and shampoo lingered on his skin and his lips were minty fresh.

"I, um, wanted to have time for getting myself ready." Grif murmured against my mouth.

I groaned. "Oh my God." His words went straight to my dick.

"Assuming you still want to do sexy stuff before we leave?"

"Definitely." I rolled from bed. "Give me ten minutes."

Grif smiled wickedly. "Hey, um, just so you know. I *may* have ordered myself a butt plug. And I *may* have it in right now."

My mouth fell open. "You have a butt plug in your ass right now?"

"No, I have a butt plug in my ear," he deadpanned.

"Don't mess with me. You just told me something that has the potential to completely short-circuit my brain *and* dick if you're being serious."

Grif smirked. "Guess you'll have to hurry in the shower and then find out for yourself."

I all but ran to the bathroom. I took the quickest shower of my life before brushing my teeth and launching my naked body back into Griffin's bed. "Let me see your ass."

He barked out a laugh. "Where's the wining? The dining? The romance? The foreplay?"

"Let me see your ass," I repeated.

Grif pulled back the blanket and my mouth watered to find him naked. He bent his knees, feet planted on the mattress, and spread his legs.

I saw the end of a black silicone anal plug. I nearly busted a nut right there. "Why did you decide to do that?"

Grif shrugged. "Figured it would help prep me *and* it could be fun to play with it. Thought it would be sexy. Do you like it?"

I swallowed hard and nodded. "When did you put it in? What's it feel like?"

"After I cleaned myself, I lubed it and slid it in. It

doesn't hurt, but I definitely know it's there. I kinda like it, but I don't think I'd wear it all the time." He blushed. "And I *really* want to know what it feels like to have *you* in me."

"Well, I aim to please, baby. You're about to find out." I crawled between his legs and took his mouth while rutting my cock against his. There was so much in our kisses. History, brotherhood, friendship, and now a mashed-up sweet, sexy, innocent curiosity we had for each other. And love. So much love. I really didn't know that I could love Griffin more than I had when he was only my brother and best friend. But having him as a partner, a lover, *my boyfriend* showed me that our original love had the capability of expanding exponentially.

He broke the kiss with a gasp and rocked his hips into mine. "I'm really worked up. Could probably come this way." He blushed and licked his lips. "But I'm dying to have you inside me. I know what it felt like to be inside you. I want you to feel that. And I want to experience what you got to last night."

"You trying to speed things along, baby?" I teased.

"God yes, Q. We've got lots of time for all types of sex, but right now I *really* want you in my ass. Please." He bit his bottom lip.

"Well, if you're going to beg." I winked and moved to his right side. "Can I play for just a minute?" I teased a finger along the end of the plug.

Grif moaned and nodded his head.

I took hold of the silicone and slowly pulled the plug

from his body halfway before sliding it back in. The way his body opened and clung to the toy heated my blood. I wanted his body open for me, clinging to me. I leaned down to suck his cock deep in my mouth while I played with the plug for a few more moments.

"Q, *please.*" Grif panted.

"Want to stop?" I tongued his cock.

"Fuck off," he huffed. "You know what I want. Stop making me wait."

I laughed and moved up to kiss him. "So bossy." Ripping open a condom and then rolling it down my length, I drizzled lube on my cock before easing the plug from Grif's ass. I teased a slick finger in and around his hole and took great pleasure in the way he threw his head back and groaned. "Grab a pillow."

Grif shoved a pillow under his ass.

No fantasy, no porn, *nothing* could have ever prepared me for the vision before me. My thick cock pressing at Grif's entrance, his body opening for me as if welcoming my invasion, his hands clenched on the sheets, and his body flushed with desire. Desire for *me.* Griffin wanted this as much as I did. He wanted this with me, not with just anybody.

I groaned as my dick slid into his heat. "Oh fuck, G."

"It's amazing, right?" He panted and shifted his hips under me. "Fuck me."

"*Dirty,* bossy bottom." I teased, but moved his legs up to my shoulders and thrust in and out of his body several times. Turning to kiss his calf, I kept one arm on his leg and gripped his cock with the other. "So hot and tight. But it's more than that. It's *seeing* my cock sliding in and out of your body. Ruined. I'm ruined for anyone else."

"Damn right you are. So am I. Never anyone else." Grif rolled his ass against me. "Fuck me. Hard."

"Are you sure?"

"Yes, please. I wanna feel your cock throbbing in my ass."

Couldn't argue with what my boy wanted. I leaned forward and let Grif's legs slide around my waist. With my arms hooked under his armpits and holding the top of his shoulders, I held tight and thrust into him hard and fast.

Griffin whimpered under me and gasped on my deepest thrust. "Oh my God, do that again."

I chuckled and kissed him. "G, I'm so close. Come for me."

He took his cock from me and pumped himself hard and fast in rhythm to my dick thrusting into him. I felt his body tense and tighten under me one second before he shouted and shot his release between us. His ass clenched and I had no hope of holding back. My orgasm ripped from me, exploding deep in his ass, my cock pulsing.

When it felt as if every bit of my life had been drained from my body, I collapsed on Griffin and panted. He wrapped his arms around my back and squeezed my ass.

"Best. Ever." I breathed hard.

"So, last night was amazing," Grif hedged.

"But?"

He kissed my head. "But, if it's okay with you, I'd *really* like to have sex like this as often as possible."

I laughed. "Baby, as much as I loved your dick in me, there is *nowhere* I'd rather be than with my cock buried deep in your pretty little ass. You've got *no* worries there."

Griffin sighed. "Another reason we're absolutely perfect together."

"Perfect." I kissed his chest before taking his face in my hands. "I. Love. You. Always and forever. Not just because of this. In addition to this. Despite this. You're mine. I'm yours. This is right. It's perfect. We are always and forever."

Griffin's eyes glistened and he nodded. "I love you, Q."

10

GRIFFIN

WE SLEPT for about an hour before rolling from bed and taking quick showers. We were spending a week with Momma, but we only packed about three changes of clothes because we could do laundry at her sister's place.

"Let's take coffee and tea with us. We'll stop for lunch in three or four hours." Quincy doctored up his own coffee and my tea in travel mugs. "Honestly, I may have been a little cocky thinking we could do a fourteen-hour drive straight through. Maybe we'll stop tonight and finish in the morning."

My stomach sank slightly. "If we can take snacks with us and maybe drive straight through that would save money on meals and a hotel." Being a full-time business major *and* cosmetology school didn't leave me time to work. I had some money for living expenses, but funds were *always* tight and I needed to save as much as possible.

"Well, if *someone* hadn't balked so much about the price of tickets, we could have flown to see Momma." Quincy kissed my cheek and handed me a mug of tea.

"Those tickets were over five hundred dollars apiece. You know I don't have that type of money." Money was a constant issue between us. Likely because I had none and Quincy had never wanted for anything.

"Max and Momma were covering the cost." Quincy shrugged. "But this way we get fourteen hours together."

I let the argument die for the time being. We gathered our bags, locked the suite, and headed to the car.

Tunes cranked up, Quincy pointed the car toward Florida and our long-ass drive.

Four hours later, I needed to pee, I was starving, and Quincy seemed ready to strangle me if I belted out one more Disney song from my playlist.

"Let's stop for lunch. And then you can drive for a while. But *I* get to pick the playlist on the next part of the drive." Quincy pulled into a sit-down type restaurant.

"Let's just get fast food," I suggested as I calculated the cost of lunch.

"Nah, I want real food." Q started to get out of the car.

"Quincy, I don't have the money for lots of pricey meals. Fast food is cheaper."

He stopped himself from opening the car door and leaned over to me. "Baby, meals are on Max. He sent money. Please, let's just eat some good food and rest a little before we head out again."

I crossed my arms over my chest. "Quincy, it's fine that *your* dad sent *you* money. I have a very limited amount of cash to work with on this trip. I'd rather be able to get an adequate lunch for five or six dollars than get water and a side salad for the same amount and then be hungry in an hour."

"G, my dad sent money for us both. You know he always includes you. He feels guilty for being gone so much of my childhood." Quincy cupped my cheek. "Not that I'm complaining. If he hadn't been gone the way he was, I wouldn't have had as much time with my brother and best friend. But he sent money for gas, lodging, and food on the way to see Momma. I think it's also partly because he feels guilty he's not been to see Momma yet. Please, let's just eat here. Save your money. You know Max won't take back anything he sent, so we may as well use it."

My stomach rumbled. I hated being in this position. On one hand, I knew Max was well-off enough that he could afford to fund our trip. I knew Max cared about me and loved his son. I knew Max wouldn't hear of accepting any of the money back. But I also felt like a complete mooch letting Q's dad pay for me. I was supposed to be a grown-up. I was supposed to be independent and paying for my own way. Yet, here I was, struggling to make ends meet and conflicted over eating at a roadside diner type place.

"Fine. We'll eat here. But I need you to listen to my concerns once we're back on the road." I knew Q would listen. I knew he'd try to understand. I also knew he wouldn't ever truly *get it*. But I had to at least try. For my own sanity.

We trooped into the restaurant and chose a back, corner table. The entire place smelled heavenly and my stomach growled again.

"I think I want every single item on the menu," Q stated as we perused the choices.

I settled on a burger and fries. Quincy ordered a sampler appetizer along with a burger and fries. I knew he expected me to share the appetizer.

"We could have gotten a burger and fries at a fast food place." I scowled.

"Yeah, but this is nicer and better. Plus, the appetizer sampler isn't available at fast food." He winked.

By the time we'd demolished our food and relaxed a little from being cooped up inside the car, Quincy took the bill and headed toward the counter.

"At least let me leave a tip," I grumbled.

"Fine, if that makes you happy, baby." Quincy smiled at me.

After restroom stops, we were back on the road. Me driving, Quincy manning the music.

"So, we'll stop again in about three hours to switch. Then we can drive about four more hours and stop for the night." Quincy spoke as he scrolled through his phone. "Looks like we'll have good hotel options. That means we'll get up in the morning and just have a three-hour drive."

I rolled my eyes. "You're kinda a steamroller in situations like this. You know that, right?"

"Huh?" Quincy looked up, brows furrowed.

"I guess you come by it honestly. Momma was always the same way. You guys get these ideas in your head and no one can stop you."

"What are you trying to stop?" Quincy continued to frown.

"I suggested a while ago that maybe we drive straight through so as to save money." I raised my brows.

"Baby, we've got the money. The drive is crazy long. There's no reason to put either of our lives in danger trying to drive straight through just to save some money." He reached for my hand. "I know money is a touchy subject for you. Why don't you tell me how you're feeling? But I need you to know that stopping for the night is a definite. We're not risking our lives."

I took a deep breath and let it out slowly. We had three hours before our next stop. Quincy was a captive audience. Even if I likely couldn't change his mind, at least I could try to express my feelings.

"First, I need to say that this," I gestured between the two of us, "is so amazing. I've fallen hard. Hook, line, and sinker as Momma would say."

I glanced at Quincy and his smile warmed me.

"I was so scared to mess up our friendship, but this has turned out to be the best decision of my life. My only regret…"

Quincy squeezed my hand. "Regret?"

"Don't interrupt." I squeezed back. "My only regret is that wc didn't take the next step sooner. I feel like we missed out on some great times by hiding our feelings and being worried we'd mess things up."

"Nah. I understand what you're saying, but we had all those years as brothers and best friends. If we'd tried to be more before now, maybe we weren't ready. Maybe it wouldn't have worked. And we've got forever together either way. It's all good." Quincy pressed the back of my hand to his lips and kissed me softly.

I thought about his words. "Yeah, I can see that."

"We've always been better together than apart. And now we have our history to build on and be *forever* better together." Quincy kissed my cheek. "You should write this shit down, I'm kinda romantic."

I snorted. "Forever better together. It's the truth. But I don't think you'll be writing for greeting cards anytime soon."

Quincy gasped and pretended to be offended.

We laughed and enjoyed a comfortable silence for the remainder of whatever song was playing.

"So that was your 'first.' What else did you want to say?" Quincy chewed on a thumbnail.

"Don't bite your nails. It's unhealthy." I used our joined hands to bat his other hand from his mouth. "I never felt like I fit in. I felt like a bother to my parents. I felt like a nuisance to the fosters before Momma. I never felt like I was a *part* of anything." I turned to catch Q's eye. "Until you. Until Momma, Pops, and you. Beyond all reason, despite my past, breaking through my hang-ups, the three of you always made me feel wanted, needed, and accepted."

"That's because you've always *been* wanted, needed, and accepted. We love you like you're blood family. Maybe even more than some blood family. *I love you.* Where you going with this, G?" Quincy worried his bottom lip.

"We're so different."

"We've had this conversation," Quincy interrupted.

"Hush. This isn't about our differences so much. It's more about me not being able to work right now and never having money. When I'm at school, it's not that hard. I've got the meal credits, credits at the commissary, pretty much everything I need. But it's scary how reliant I am on the school money and credits. If I was on my own, I wouldn't survive more than a week. I wish I could work so I could have a little bit of a cushion. I have the cheapest phone package and have to rely on people sharing their WiFi with me. When I'm out places, I have to make sure I'm not using up data."

"Baby, I can always help with bills and things. I know we don't have bills at school so much, but I can help with other stuff. Let me get you a better phone package. Let me help with a better car."

I knew Quincy never understood why I insisted on still driving the junker I bought in high school. "Stop! Don't you get it? I want to be able to do all of that for myself. I *hate* being a mooch, relying on others."

Quincy gaped. "G, you're not a mooch. *No one* has ever felt that way. Ever."

"I've never once been able to take care of myself. I was reliant on my parents. I was reliant on the fosters. I was reliant on Momma and Pops. For a lot of the homes, I was just a paycheck. For Momma and Pops I never felt that way, but at least they got paid for taking care of me until they adopted me. After that? I was just another financial burden."

"Oh my God, baby. How can you even think that? Momma and Pops *wanted* to adopt you. They *loved* you. They were so proud of you. You were never a burden on them. No one would have ever expected you to take care of yourself. Momma and Pops didn't take you in thinking you'd one day pay them back. You were just a kid!"

"Yeah. I was a kid. *Then*. Now I'm a grown-up and still not able to take care of myself. At least as a foster kid, I brought them some money from the state. But now Momma's buying me expensive gifts, Max is funding a road trip, and you're offering to pay my phone bill. I feel like a complete loser mooch."

"Grif, I'm so sorry you feel this way. I don't know how to make you understand. Momma and Pops *wanted* you. They took pride in taking care of you. My dad isn't super emotional, but he considers you as much his son as me. Me offering to help you is just that. An offer to help. You know why? Because I know you'd help me in a heartbeat when you're in the position to be able to." He kissed the back of my hand. "And one day, you *will* be in that position. You're not always going to be broke, relying on scholarships and credits through the school. You won't always need my dad to pay for a road trip. Hell, *I* won't always need my dad to pay for a road trip." He turned in his seat so he could see me better. "We may be *grown*, but we're not expected to be one hundred percent self-reliant right now. We're in school. We can do as much on our own as possible, but we have resources to help us through. And that makes us lucky. One day, when we're better off financially, we'll be able to help some young adults like ourselves. Until then, we accept the assistance we're given and be grateful for it."

I sighed and attempted to loosen my grip on the steering wheel. What Quincy said made sense. Mostly. But it didn't make the little voice in my head stop whispering that I was a loser, a mooch, someone who couldn't even support myself.

"Maybe if I'd grown up with money readily available, this wouldn't be so hard. But I've never had money." I shook my head. "Don't get me wrong. I'm not saying money is everything. I think there are many happy people who don't have much. I was so scared and unhappy with my parents. We had no money. I don't know if money would have made anything better. I felt loved and happy with Momma and Pops. I might not have had my own money then, but even at a young age, I knew money made things easier."

Quincy rubbed my hand with his thumb and let me keep talking.

"Your entire family has always been beyond generous with me. I guess I've always had the idea that, once I was officially an adult, I'd be able to repay or show my own generosity. But here I am, legal and all that, and I'm still having to think about the price of a pair of shoes or lunch at a restaurant or paying my phone bill." I smiled softly. "I know it's hard for you to understand."

"It kinda is. I've never really had to worry about money. It's not like I got every single thing I wanted, but *needs* were taken care of and wants were usually allowed. Honestly, I'm sort of worried about being on my own. Eventually, my dad and Momma will stop supporting me. The scholarships will run out. I'll be employed; dear Lord, I pray I'm employed. I'll be expected to pay rent or a house payment, bills, groceries, living expenses. And I don't really know how to do any of that." Quincy shrugged. "So, you may be feeling like a loser right now, but just know that I'm worried I'll turn into a loser once I have to do this all on my own."

"Awww, I never knew you worried about that." It was unusual to see Q vulnerable. But it made him all the more loveable to me. "And no worries, babe.

You've got a business major *and* future hair and makeup artist to the stars as your *forever*. We've got this."

"Yeah?" Quincy grinned. "I like the sound of that. You'll make sure I'm being smart financially? Maybe be my sugar daddy if I can't land a job?"

"Oh fuck, no. But I'll be sure to help you get a job. And help you budget your money. We can be in it together," I assured.

"And we've already figured out we're better together."

"Forever." I kissed his hand as we pulled into the rest stop.

* * *

FOUR HOURS LATER, Quincy whipped the car into a popular hotel chain. He laid back against the seat and moaned. "Oh my God, I'm dead. No way I could drive any longer." He turned and pointed out the window. "Let's check in and then we can walk over to that Denny's. I'm starving."

I was so tired, I didn't even object. I wanted *out* of the car. I wanted food. I needed a shower. And I needed sleep.

We got checked in. I tried not to feel bad when Q ran his credit card for the room. I knew Max paid the balance every month.

Once we got our bags to the room, Quincy scanned a few delivery menus.

"You want to walk to the Denny's?" He waved the menus. "Or we can order delivery."

"Honestly? If delivery means I can get in the shower sooner rather than later, I say go with delivery."

Q laughed. "Totally agree. You shower and I'll order."

Forty-five minutes later, we'd both showered and the food was spread out in front of us like a feast at the little hotel table.

"Pizza, Chinese, *and* burgers and fries?" I laughed. "Hungry?"

"Famished." Quincy pulled me into a fierce hug. "But there's a method to my madness. I figure we can eat the burgers and fries and some Chinese *now*. Warm up Chinese and pizza in the morning. And any extra pizza can go with us as snacks for the rest of the drive."

"Genius. My boyfriend is a genius." I kissed him with a hard smack against his lips. "We should try to head out by nine in the morning, yeah?" I grabbed a fry and chomped on it as we settled in to eat.

"Yeah, I told Momma to expect us a little after noon." Q took a giant bite of a burger and groaned. "So good."

"So, I never met Momma's sister. What's she like?" I tore into my own cheeseburger. It really was delicious. But possibly only because I was exhausted and starving.

"Well, Aunt Mae is actually Great Aunt Maebelle. But she doesn't acknowledge her age so don't mention the *Great* Aunt part. And if you value your life, you will *never* call her Maebelle. She claims she nixed the Belle part when she was two and refused to speak to anyone who called her by her full name." Quincy chuckled. "But Momma swears that the family called her Maebelle her entire childhood and it wasn't until college that Mae stopped using the Belle."

"Marlene and Maebelle. That's cute. Marlene and Mae." I shook my head. "Sorry, I can't do Marlene. *Momma* and Mae. That's better. I can handle that."

We finished our food and cleaned up. Quincy deemed the pizza would be fine to sit out over night as long as the box was closed. The leftover Chinese was squeezed into the tiny fridge. I gathered the trash.

"We should make sure we're packed and ready so all we have to do is shower and dress before heading out." Quincy hung a shirt in the closet.

When we finally flopped onto the king-sized bed, I wondered if I'd ever been so tired.

"This bed is amazing. So big."

"A lot different from our squished together twins back home." I smiled at the memory and my heart warmed.

"I know we're both exhausted. But I also know we may not get much alone time at Aunt Mae's." Quincy turned to his side and propped his head on his elbow.

"Just what are you suggesting, Mr. Sanders?" I turned to face him and ran my hand down his side. My dick was immediately on board with whatever he had in mind.

"Maybe we fool around a little before sleep?" Q raised a brow.

"I mean, we've got this amazing bed. It would be a shame to waste it, right? Plus, as tired as I am, I still feel a little wound up."

"Well then, by all means, allow me to unwind you." He pulled me close and kissed me hungrily.

I threw a leg over Q's hips and moaned as our cocks rocked together. "Naked. We should be naked."

Quincy pulled back just enough to rip his shirt over his head before he grabbed the hem of mine and tore it over my head. We fumbled together to push our sweats down until the material was kicked to the side and forgotten. Q rolled to the side of the bed and fumbled through his bag. He quickly produced lube and a condom.

I watched, heart and cock pumping the same rhythm, as he ripped open the condom and rolled it down his length.

"Face away from me." Quincy's demand took my breath away.

I rolled to my right side, facing my back to him.

The snap of the lube opening made my dick jerk.

And then Quincy was pressed against my back, his strong heat surrounding me. He kissed my neck and nibbled at my ear as his cock pressed into my ass. "Lift your leg." Q hefted my left leg up and back a little to drape over his left leg. "This okay?" His whispered concern for me warmed my heart.

"Yeah, very okay." My breath hitched when his cock head pushed against my entrance. "Go slow, little sore."

"Too sore? We don't have to." Quincy paused and kissed my neck.

"No, I want to. Just soft and slow tonight, yeah?"

"Mmmm, that sounds amazing," Q growled at my ear. He pressed slowly into my body.

The initial sting faded and allowed for a pleasurable heat to fill me. "So big and hot," I panted.

"You're so damn tight, G," Quincy gritted out.

I turned my head toward him and let Q's tongue plunge into my mouth, let his lips own mine. All while his cock slid slow and deep in and out of my body.

His right arm was under me and his hand snaked up to toy with my nipples while his left hand trailed from my hip to stroke my dick. He ran his thumb through my wet slit before gripping me again. I thrust into his fist in the same slow rhythm as his cock pumped into my ass.

Our bodies, united as one, were lost in a haze of lovemaking for several moments until Quincy growled, "I'm gonna come, gonna fill this pretty little ass."

I whimpered and my balls drew up tight. I moved my left leg to the mattress and twisted my hips in such a way that Quincy was more on top as he pumped into me. The change in angle had him brushing all the right spots and I saw stars. I cried out as my release erupted from me, my head thrown back as Q kissed my neck.

Quincy thrust deep one last time and groaned as his cock throbbed hot and hard in my ass. He continued to pump into me as he rode out his orgasm until he collapsed on me, breathing hard.

"Yeah, we can't do that at Aunt Mae's," I panted.

"Definitely not," Quincy agreed. "Maybe they'll go play Bingo or something one night. Or we can be extra quiet with locked doors and blowjobs."

"And we'll just have to look forward to being back in our private suite." I sighed as Quincy pulled from my body. "Can you imagine how much it would have sucked to be placed with a different roommate?"

Quincy shuddered. "So terrible. But I get you all to myself for all four years. Perfect."

"Thanks to Momma."

"We really should thank her again. She's allowed for her sons to cohabitate and fuck each other's brains out any time of the day." Quincy winked.

"Probably best to avoid mentioning that. I know she wanted us together and happy. But I'm thinking she doesn't want to hear about our sex life." I chuckled.

Quincy rolled from the bed and grabbed a couple washcloths. "True that. Although, with Momma, you never really know."

We cleaned up and climbed under the fluffy softness of the comforter. Quincy pulled me into his arms and kissed the top of my head. "I love you, G."

"Love you," I whispered against his chest.

* * *

THE NEXT MORNING, after showers and leftover Chinese, we hit the road.

"Three hours!" Quincy pumped a fist. "I'm ready for this drive to be over."

"I can't believe how much warmer it is down here. I'm glad I brought shorts and t-shirts." I held my hand out the window and enjoyed the warmth of the sun on my face.

"I'm thinking Momma will stay with Mae from now on. No need for her to be anywhere else." Quincy eased the car into interstate traffic. "We could make this our normal winter break destination. Get time with Momma plus warm weather and the chance to relax between semesters."

"That sounds amazing. Build new traditions with Momma and for us." I loved the thought of set visits with Momma and yearly vacations with Q. "And, one day, we'll be able to pay for it ourselves." I teased and then laughed when Quincy's face wrinkled.

"Yeah, that sounds amazing." He deadpanned.

We chatted about the different trees and roadside vegetation, the different restaurants and shops and gas stations we saw along the way—so many were new to us—and what we wanted to do with the week we were spending with Momma.

In no time at all, we pulled into the small neighborhood where Aunt Mae and Momma lived. A few twists and turns through the community and we pulled up to the correct address. Momma and Mae sat on the front porch smiling broadly.

"Wow." Quincy sighed. "Really hard to see Momma without Pops, but she looks healthy and happy. And knowing she's as excited to see us as we are to see her is nice."

I swallowed thickly. "Aside from Max, Pops was the only *real* father figure I ever had. I wish he could be sitting there with her." My eyes stung. "But she *does* look okay, like she's adjusted well."

"Okay, let's not get all teary-eyed before we go say hello." Quincy leaned over and kissed me.

"Oh wow, you think Aunt Mae is okay with us together?" It wasn't a thought I'd had until that very moment.

"You actually think Momma would live with someone who didn't accept her boys exactly the way they are?" Quincy rolled his eyes.

I laughed, relieved. "True. I don't know what I was thinking."

We hefted our bags from the car and headed to the porch. The small home had three steps to the porch, but a ramp was also available if needed. The porch was covered in a fake grass type carpet and Aunt Mae had several plants decorating the area.

"My boys," Momma croaked and pulled us both into the tightest, longest hug she'd given us since the day she left us at college. "Oh Lord, it's so good to see you. I've been needin' a little Q and G something fierce."

When we finally pulled apart, the three of us were sniffling and wiping our eyes, Momma motioned to her sister. "Q, you remember Aunt Mae."

Quincy stepped forward and hugged his aunt.

"Griffin, I know you've heard of Aunt Mae

throughout the years, but after she moved to Florida when Quincy was nine, we really didn't get to see her much." Momma stopped and tapped her chin as if recalling something. "I guess Pops and I came down a couple times, but we never had you boys with us." She waved away her thought. "That's neither here nor there, *this* is the infamous Aunt Mae you've heard so much about."

I walked into Aunt Mae's hug and truly felt as if I'd been approved, welcomed, loved, and *wanted* within seconds of her arms wrapping around me.

"I never got to have children," Aunt Mae stated as she patted my cheek. "But having Quincy and you as my nephews has always made me feel like I got to be a surrogate mother. I just hate that we never really got to spend much time together."

"No worries about that Aunt Mae," Q interrupted. "Griffin and I are already planning vacations to see you and Momma on each winter break."

"Well now, that sounds downright perfect." Mae beamed.

"Let's not be too hasty in skipping over Spring Break and summertime." Momma stood with her hands on her hips.

Quincy and I glanced at each other and shrugged.

"As long as jobs and money and schedules allow for it, we could make at least one of those work." Quincy picked up his bag where he'd dropped it on the floor.

I did the same.

"Well, if you two knuckleheads," Momma started,

but she looked directly at me, "would allow Max to pay for plane tickets, the trip would be much easier."

Quincy laughed and I blushed.

"Fourteen hours in a car with Quincy? Nah, it was a breeze." I tucked my arm through Q's.

"Hey, it was actually fun. Aside from Grif's questionable song choices. And he's not *as* great at driving as I am."

I elbowed him and he grunted.

"But we enjoyed lots of conversation time." Quincy kissed the side of my head.

"Well, I think a plane would be easier. Plus, it would get you here quicker." Momma swung the front door open and ushered us inside.

"Thanks for all the Christmas gifts, Momma. You went *way* beyond what was necessary, but the items were amazing." I kissed her cheek.

"Yes, the gifts were so great. Thank you." Quincy hugged her close to his side as we followed Aunt Mae.

Mae directed us toward the back of the house. "Now, Marlene assured me you two would be comfortable rooming together. She took the guest room, but this is the den. We outfitted it with a nice bed. You should have plenty of room. And the door locks."

Quincy and I appeared to both make the decision to ignore the insinuation and simply walked into the room and tossed our bags down. The room was just slightly larger than my bedroom in the suite, but a full-size bed fit easily. Plants adorned every nook and cranny of the room. The dark wood paneling spoke of the age of the home. But the mauve carpet hinted that at least the carpeting had been replaced somewhat recently.

"Oh wow, this is great. Thank you so much. I hope it wasn't too much trouble to set us up in here." I sat gently on the soft bed.

"Nonsense. I don't do anything if it's too much trouble." Aunt Mae waved off my concern.

"Are you boys hungry?" Momma gestured toward the door.

"Starving." Quincy rushed out of the room.

"Yes, we are hungry," I agreed with a smile and followed Quincy.

Momma and Mae bustled easily together around the kitchen and produced four plates. Turkey, ham, and roast beef sub sandwiches, chips, baked beans, and coleslaw.

"Water, sweet tea, coffee, or juice?" Momma asked.

"I made unsweet tea, too." Mae held up a smaller pitcher.

"Oh, I'll take unsweet." I grabbed a glass and filled it with ice.

"Eeew, I'll take sweet tea. The only way tea should ever be consumed." Quincy filled his own glass with ice and bumped my hip.

"I like hot tea sweet, but iced tea I like unsweet." I shrugged and poured my drink.

The four of us sat down at the table like we'd been doing it our whole lives and tore into our food. Okay,

Quincy and I tore into our food. Momma and Mae were slightly more civilized.

"This is the best coleslaw I've ever eaten." I shoveled more into my mouth.

"And the baked beans?" Quincy moaned and glanced Heaven-ward. "So good. Don't get beans like this back at school."

"How in the world does a simple lunchmeat sandwich taste so good?" I wondered aloud around a bite before popping a chip into my mouth.

"Oh dear, it's worse than I feared." Momma held a hand to her mouth.

Aunt Mae nodded. "They've been starved at school."

"We've got a week to feed them properly. My sweet, sweet deprived boys, what meals would you like while you're here?" Momma took both of our hands.

Quincy and I stared at each other across the table. Had we been starved? No. Did Momma *really* think we'd been going without food? No. Well, probably not. But did the thought of our favorite homemade meals appeal? Yes. Hell, yes.

Our requests included chicken and noodles with mashed potatoes, baked macaroni and cheese, fried chicken, cinnamon rolls, beef roast with potatoes and carrots, and homemade rolls.

The request of cinnamon rolls reminded Momma that we'd attempted our own Christmas Day breakfast and lunch. By the time we finished telling the story of the burned chicken and veggies, Momma and Mae were laughing so hard they were crying.

"But the cinnamon rolls were amazing." Quincy defended.

I nodded. "They really were. *Almost* as good as yours."

"Boys, are you wanting a nap or want to see the beach?" Mae began to clear the table.

Quincy and I jumped up to help.

"I see you raised them right, Marlene." Mae smiled as she watched us clean up.

"Only way to do it. No sons of mine are going to sit around and let a female clean the kitchen." Momma nodded proudly.

"We'd be sitting around waiting for a *very* long time if either of us were expecting a female to show up and clean our messes back at school." Quincy threw an arm around my shoulders and kissed the side of my head. "We split the chores and keep things nice and neat just the way Momma taught us."

I threw away the last of the trash as Quincy put the condiments back in the fridge. "I'm not all that sleepy. I'd love to see the beach."

"Perfect. Momma and I have an umbrella and lounges reserved. We'll relax out of the sun while you two explore and play." Mae gave the table a quick wipe with a damp paper towel.

Thirty minutes later, Quincy and I were covered in sunscreen and the four of us trooped three blocks from the house to find a lovely little beach. The December weather averaged seventy-one degrees and we'd lucked out with an above-average day. The sun was shining brightly and the breeze was warm as we approached the sandy beach. Salt and seaweed scents mixed on the air.

"It's semi-private in that only the surrounding communities can access it. So, it's never completely empty, but you won't have party kids or little ones underfoot." Mae spread a towel on a lounge chair.

Momma laid her own towel out. "You can go all the way to the yellow flag in both directions. If you go too far either way you'll run into public beach in one direction and private beach in the other. So, stay between the yellow flags. Oh, and the water is warmer right now than average, but it's still pretty chilly."

Q and I walked down toward the water. While I'd seen beaches and even walked beaches, the water or weather had always been too cold to get in. And, honestly, getting *in* the ocean water wasn't something I'd ever longed to do.

"Want to see how cold it is?" Q held his hand out to me.

I shivered and took his hand. "I'll go up to my knees. Maybe waist. But no deeper. The ocean kind freaks me out, especially the deeper water. And if it's cold, no thanks."

We let the small waves overtake our feet and gasped at how cool the water was. But soon, we adjusted and ventured a bit farther into the water. The warm sun and soft breeze mixed with the cool water was actually kind of the perfect combination.

"Let's walk to the yellow flag." Quincy pointed to the flag north of us. "Maybe find some crabs or shells?"

Quincy kept my hand in his as we wandered the beach. We meandered from water to dry sand and back as we walked.

"I think the constant sand everywhere would get annoying, but I kinda love the thought of being so close to a beach." I grabbed a pretty shell and rubbed my thumb over it.

"Yeah, let's plan on having a beach house when we're both employed." Quincy bent down to retrieve a smooth black stone.

"Oh, I like that plan. Let's also plan on a mountain getaway." I added another shell to my growing collection.

"Of course. We'll live in the city or at least close enough for the best jobs. But we'll vacation in the mountains and at the beach." Quincy picked up another stone. "We should take these home. I bet we can make some cool decorative jars with shells and stones."

With that in mind, we gathered more shells and smooth beach stones. Once we reached the yellow flag, we retraced our steps until we got to Momma and Mae. Depositing our collection with them, Quincy and I took off to the flag south of us.

We took time to build a small sand castle with a moat. It looked more like a sand mound with a moat, but we were sure to adorn our creation with shells, sea grass, and a stick.

"Oh, we need to put our names and the date in the sand and take a picture." I grabbed a larger stick and used it to write *Quincy* and *Griffin* along with a heart and the year beneath our names. "Take a picture."

Quincy insisted on getting a pic of the sand writing in a selfie of the two of us. Then he wanted us kissing with the sign behind us. Both of these pictures required an odd angle, but turned out nice. Finally, he snapped a photo of just the words before we finished our walk to the flag.

When we arrived back at the umbrella, Momma and Mae were ready to head back.

"You boys can stay if you'd like." Momma shook out her towel and folded it before stuffing it in her beach bag.

"Nah, I think we've had enough beach. Would rather spend time with you." Quincy gathered our shells and stones.

"I've got some jars you can put those in." Mae gestured to the shells as we left the beach.

"Perfect way to remember your first Florida beach as a couple." Momma put her arms around both of us.

"We got a great picture of our names in the sand, too." I knew without a doubt that I'd have the pictures printed and likely put them in frames. They would make a perfect little trio of photographs to decorate the suite. And one day, our home. My heart fluttered.

The next few days were a jumble of laughter, love, relaxing, and adventure. Momma and Mae kept us busy with stories, shopping, and sight-seeing. They also kept us well-fed. The meals never stopped. Momma even bought us a large cooler which she planned to pack with leftovers and ice packs for our trip back. She claimed the cooler and ice would keep the leftovers safe for reheating once we were back at school as long as we transferred from cooler to refrigerator as soon as we got to the suite. The thought of noodles, mashed potatoes, roast, veggies, and macaroni and cheese for meals once we were back home brought a smile to my face. The fact that Momma filled an entire bread bag with homemade yeast rolls was just icing on the cake.

The day before we were scheduled to leave, Momma bustled into the kitchen where Quincy and I were eating a snack of fried chicken. "I've got an offer for you boys, but only if you're comfortable with it."

We stopped eating and listened.

"I spread Pops ashes when I first got here."

My heart ached at the mention of Pops.

"But I saved a small urn for each of you. If you'd like, we can go out on a boat tonight and you can scatter his ashes. But it's up to you."

Quincy reached for my hand. "What do you think?"

I nodded. "I'd like to. Maybe sunset?" I turned to Momma. "Could we maybe scatter one urn and take the other one with us?"

"Of course, that's a great idea."

So, we headed toward a dock about thirty minutes before sunset. A very kind older gentleman assisted Momma, Quincy, and I aboard and promised to get us to a perfect spot for scattering ashes.

As the sun began to set, Quincy and I stood

shoulder to shoulder with Momma behind us, her hands on us, and said a few words.

"I miss you Pops." Quincy's words were gruff. "Thank you for raising me and being such a good role model. I appreciate your wisdom and patience." He sprinkled some of the ashes into the water.

Tears ran down my face as I took the urn. "You were the only *real* dad I ever had. You accepted me the moment I stepped foot in your home. You taught me how to change oil in a car, even though I'll probably always go to a shop." I laughed and sniffed. "You taught me how to mow the lawn, but I plan to hire that out."

We all laughed. Pops was a do-it-yourself type guy. I appreciated him teaching me, but I didn't find the same joy in oil changes and lawn mowing that he did.

"I miss your quiet sense of humor. I miss watching TV with you. I miss the way your eyes sparkled for Momma. I miss your love and support for Quincy and me." I sprinkled more ashes.

Momma sniffled behind us. "Don't you boys ever think that Pops' isn't still loving and supporting you." She took the urn. "Duane, I miss you. But I'm okay. And I'll continue to be okay until the day we meet again. Thank you for being my partner, my support, my joy. I'd love to see you again, but I've got our boys to think of. I'll be busy loving them, supporting them, and watching them continue to grow into amazing men. I figure I need to hang around for the engagement, the wedding, and maybe a couple pets or babies at least. So, you keep on loving us and holding a place for me. I'll see you soon." Momma sprinkled the last of the ashes over the water.

The three of us spent the boat ride home in quiet contemplation.

As we neared the docks, Quincy took our hands. "Thank you. That was hard and a bit more emotional than I was ready for, but it brought some closure. I loved that man."

I could only nod and sniff my nose.

"Well, there's one last thing I'd like to talk to you boys about." Momma took our hands as we left the boat. "Would you like to grab some coffee or tea and sit on the back patio?"

Apprehension filled my gut, but I agreed. "Hot tea would be perfect."

Quincy squeezed my hand. "Coffee sounds good."

We made our way back to Aunt Mae's and fixed our coffees and tea before settling in on the patio. It was a beautiful little spot. Tropical plants galore, tiki torches providing some light and bug protection, and strings of pink flamingo lights adding a splash of color.

Before we had headed to the patio, I grabbed Quincy. "Do you know what this is about?"

He shook his head and shrugged.

Momma took a sip of her coffee. "Oh, that's good. Perfect temperature, perfect sweetness."

Quincy and I anxiously sipped our own drinks and waited.

Momma cleared her throat. "I may be out of line. No, not so much out of line. I may be reading into things too much. But I get the feeling that money may be an issue between the two of you. Am I right?"

Quincy glanced at me, eyes wide as if to say *I'll leave this one up to you.*

I rolled my eyes. "Okay, I'm a little sensitive about money. More specifically my *lack* of money and relying on others."

"That's what I thought. Griffin, you've always been that way; Pops and I could always see it." Momma took another drink. "But I need you to hear this. Pops and I came from completely different financial backgrounds. But the moment Duane and I became a couple, a *team,* we immediately agreed to stop looking at our money situation as separate and unequal. We were together, *united,* and we pooled our resources. Over the years, throughout many different situations and circumstances, there were times when one of us brought in more money and times when the other one brought in the most. But we never looked at it as one bringing in more; we supported each other in ways that went far beyond money. Griffin, there will be times when you're making more money; there will be times when Quincy is making more. In the best of times, you'll both be making a good amount. In the worst of times, you'll both struggle. But it's not about the money. It's about the support, the love, the teamwork, and the unity. It's about being wise stewards of your money. It's about smart investments, planning ahead, knowing when to save versus when to splurge. Money should never be something you allow to separate you.

Your love must be stronger than that." She took a final swig of her coffee. "I hope you're both hearing me."

Quincy nodded. I knew he wanted to pipe up with something like, *That's what I've been telling him.* But he was smarter than that.

I nodded. "I hear you. It's hard. I have a lot of issues surrounding money. But I promise I'll try." I reached for Quincy's hand. "I'll try."

He kissed my hand. "That's all I can ask for."

11

QUINCY

WE'D BEEN BACK in classes for about three weeks when Griffin anxiously asked me if I'd attend a party at his cosmetology school.

"It's not a fancy affair. Kind of a mixer, get to know each other and share our school with our friends/partners while sharing our friends/partners with our school family." He chewed his lip. "You don't *have* to go. I can go alone. Or skip it." He shrugged. "I just sort of wanted to get dressed up and introduce you to my school friends. And they all want to meet you since I talk about you constantly."

I kissed him. "Of course, I'll go. Sounds great."

We spent all of Saturday afternoon getting ready. I had convinced Grif to let me buy us both new clothes for the event by arguing that if I was going with him, I wanted to wear something new and nice. After four hours at the mall, we came home with new clothes *and* shoes.

"Okay, I'm doing make-up. Do you want to wear any?" Griffin asked as he began to spread out his brushes and supplies.

"Yeah, I'm down. Maybe not as much as Halloween, but you can highlight my best features." I batted my lashes.

He spent about thirty minutes working his magic on my face and I left looking and feeling amazing. My skin was dewy and glowing, my eyes lined just enough to make them pop, and my lashes were to die for.

An hour later, Griffin emerged from the bathroom like a damn cover model. His entire face was a work of art and his hair styled perfectly. "You ready to get dressed?"

I walked over to him and pulled him into a tight hug. "Mmmm, if it wouldn't mess up both our faces, I'd say we need to get *undressed* first." I nibbled at his neck.

"Later. After the party you can undress me." Grif laughed and gave me a soft shove.

I went to my room and pulled on my new clothes. Dark, almost black wash jeans, a plaid button-up shirt of light blues, navy, and shades of red, a navy blazer that lent itself a little more toward casual than dressy, and navy fashion sneakers. I ran a brush over my hair, spritzed a bit of cologne, checked my eyeliner, and went to the living room to wait for Griffin.

My heart nearly stopped when he finally came out of

his room. His outfit was one I would have never thought to put together, but of course, Grif made it work. Oh God, did he make it work. My mouth watered.

Dark wash skinny jeans, a dark denim button-up with the sleeves cuffed up over the arms of a dark blazer, a thin scarf, and ankle boots. Griffin smiled and strutted through the suite as if on a catwalk. "What do you think?" He posed and threw a sexy, sultry glance over his shoulder.

"Gorgeous."

Griffin wrapped his arms around my neck. "You're looking fah-bulous too, *dah-ling*." He kissed me. "Thank you for the new outfit. We didn't *need* new clothes, but I'm not going to say it wasn't fun. And I kinda *love* my new stuff."

"You're welcome. Let's go. I want to meet your friends." I took his hand as we left the suite.

Griffin's cosmetology school was about a mile from campus. On a nice day, we probably would have walked. But it was winter on the east coast so we took my car. Not only was it cold, but I knew Grif would wrinkle his nose at getting his new boots wet.

When we reached the school, I snagged a parking spot and leaned over to kiss Grif's cheek. "I'm a little nervous. What if they don't like me?"

He laughed. "It doesn't matter if *they* don't like you. We've all just sort of become a big ol' family so we wanted to introduce the important people in our lives to the whole crew."

We met on the sidewalk and joined hands.

"So, I'll introduce you to everyone. Don't mention if it's a name I complain about at home." Griffin bumped my hip with his. "Some are more annoying than others, but we're in this for the long haul. We'll probably hang with Taylor, Lyndsay, and Sarah the most. They are the ones I'm with most of the day. Probably won't spend too much time with Josh and Scott. They are kinda cliquey. If Dani is here, we'll hang with him. He's cool. Pretty much the only guy I'd consider an actual friend here."

"Babe, I'm just here to meet your friends and spend the evening with you." I pulled the door to the school building open and held it for Griffin.

Thirty minutes later, we'd eaten some hors d'oeuvres, had some drinks, and met most of Griffin's classmates plus their guests. There was absolutely no way I'd keep everyone straight in my head, but I knew Taylor and her boyfriend, Lane. Lyndsay and her sister, Lara. And Sarah with her girlfriend, Reneé. We had said hello to Josh and his boyfriend, Jason, plus Scott and their boyfriend, Jeremy. And I wasn't *at all* sure if I had the names right let alone the pairings correct. But I smiled and said hello and enjoyed being introduced as Griffin's boyfriend.

"Oh, there's Dani." Griffin pulled me toward a very attractive man with perfectly tousled hair, stylishly ripped skinny jeans, a white button up with the sleeves rolled to mid-forearm, and black leather ankle boots with just enough of a heel to bring him right about to my shoulder.

"Dani, this is my boyfriend Quincy. Q, this is Daniel, but we mostly call him Dani." Griffin gestured between us.

Dani and I shook hands and the three of us found a table.

"You guys want more food or drinks?" I asked.

They both nodded and Griffin kissed my cheek. "Thanks, babe."

When I returned with drinks and a plate of finger food, Grif and Dani were laughing about an older client they'd worked on last week.

"Oh my God, when she reached up and tried to roll her own perm rod, I thought I was going to have to keep you from strangling her." Griffin wiped his eyes.

"I was thinking, 'Bitch, if you think you can wrap and roll your whole head, be my guest.'" Dani smiled at me as he took the drink I offered.

Griffin made room for me next to him. I spent the next thirty minutes simultaneously watching the love of my life absolutely bloom right before my eyes and fighting the sinking feeling in my stomach that being with me was holding Grif back. The thought hit me somewhere between the way G's eyes lit up when he was talking about a certain makeup technique he was excited to learn and the way he sighed as he and Dani talked about dance.

"Girl, you've *got* to come audition for the tour this spring. Auditions are in spring, then practice, then the tour is all summer." Dani swirled his drink. "We've all seen you dance here, I *know* you're a natural talent."

"Nah, that's not in the cards for me right now. Couple years ago? Maybe. In the future? I don't know. But it's not what I'm focused on right now." Grif smiled at me and leaned into my side. "We've got spring and summer plans."

Dani waved him off, but I didn't miss the knowing glance he shot my way. They switched to other topics and their excitement continued. Makeup brushes, toners, the latest funny client story. I excused myself and went outside to get a breath of fresh air.

Before I returned to the party, I watched the scene from outside the large window.

Grif laughing, telling stories, animated like I'd never seen him. He was one hundred percent in his element. Was being with me keeping him from pursuing a career in dance? Was I holding him back? Would he be better off with someone like Dani? Or Josh or Scott? Men who could be as immersed in his training, in his passion, and in his love for the cosmetology business just as much as he was?

My heart plummeted to my stomach. I didn't like the answer I was being shown, but I saw the answer all too clearly.

Our differences weren't *bad*. But maybe all of our differences weren't allowing Griffin to grow and become the amazing success I knew he was going to be.

My eyes stung as I watched him and Dani start dancing with several of their classmates.

It would be selfish to keep him tethered to me when he so clearly deserved to be let loose to soar.

But my heart ached at the thought of letting him go, even though it seemed like the right thing to do.

* * *

"HEY, THERE YOU ARE." Griffin wrapped his arms around my neck and kissed me. "I thought you got lost." My cheeks were still cold from standing outside; Grif's warm lips tingled against my skin.

"Yeah, sorry. Got distracted by an email from Coach."

"You ready to go home?" Grif waved to a couple of people as they headed for the door. "I'm tired. I want to snuggle into your bed and watch movies."

"Sure. Let's go." My heart and head hurt as I contemplated how to address my concerns.

By the time we reached campus and pulled up to our building, I felt as if I was going to puke. I knew what I *needed* to do for Griffin's sake, but it wasn't something I wanted to do at all. Our history, our friendship, our love, all of it was in the balance.

"Babe, what's wrong? You're super quiet." Grif locked the suite door behind him before he followed me to the kitchen.

"I think maybe this has been a mistake and we should break up." Okay, blurting the words out like that hadn't been part of my plan and was likely the dumbest thing I could have possibly done.

Grif snorted. "What? Did you slip rum in your Coke tonight?"

"Babe, I saw your eyes light up when you talked to Dani," I began.

"*Dani*? Wait, is this a jealousy thing?"

"No, not really. Do I wish you and I could talk about our interests as animatedly as you and Dani? Sort of, yes. But it's more about the way you were completely in your element, alive, totally immersed, so excited. You turned down a dance audition and tour. Because of what? A trip to Florida with me? Baby, I can't let you be hidden and stuck here with me when you have so much more you can do."

Griffin crossed his arms and glared at me. "So, you think that because *you* aren't into dance and hair and makeup that you need to, what? *Let me go*? Is that what this is? *If you love it, let it go. If it comes back to you, it was meant to be.* Something like that? You're talking about ending a brotherhood, a friendship, a relationship that dates back almost a decade all because you can't talk perms? Or contour brushes verses stippling brushes verses highlighter brushes? Or a pixie cut verses a bob verses a layered crop?" Grif's volume increased as his words continued. "Should I be the all-valiant hero and martyr and break up with you because I don't know or care much about the difference between a touch-down, a field-goal, a three-pointer, or a homerun? We should break up and throw away something beautiful and perfect because I'd rather dance than play in a three-on-three tournament? So, all this time when you've told me our differences didn't matter, was it a lie?"

"Of course not!" I reached for him but he held his

hand up.

"So, I can't worry about our differences. I can't be concerned that we don't have a ton in common when it comes to our likes and hobbies. I can't worry that you maybe would like a sportier, more athletic boyfriend to spend your time with." Griffin rubbed a hand over his face and laughed humorlessly. "But you, *you* can see me talking with school friends about school-related topics and interests, and all of a sudden The Great and All-Knowing Quincy can decide that you're holding me back and need to set me free?"

My eyes glistened with unshed tears. "I'm just worried I'm keeping you from being all you can be. You're going to be a huge success. You're going to soar." I looked to the floor. "And I don't want to be the one keeping you from that."

Griffin rolled his eyes. "I'm not a God damn bird, Q. You're not clipping my wings or chaining me down." He slapped his hands against my chest. "You need to take some deep breaths and rethink this entire evening. I'm going to take a shower."

He turned on his heel and walked to the bathroom.

I stood in the kitchen and replayed all that had just been said.

Was I being dumb? Or was I right to think Grif would be better able to reach for the stars with someone who understood his dreams more than me?

I shook my head and wandered to my room. Ten minutes later, I was in running clothes.

"Hey G, I'm going for a run." I knocked on the

bathroom door.

By the time I'd run a mile and returned to our suite for a shower, I found Griffin in my room with a stack of large poster-size boards.

"Sit down." He glared at me and pointed at the bed.

I sat.

"First, I need you to know why I'm not interested in that dance tour." He placed the posters on my desk and propped a hand on his hip. "Number one, the director has a bad reputation. Number two, I plan on taking classes this summer. Number three, I plan to have a job this summer. Number four, I've seen the group going on tour, they aren't fabulous. Number five, I want to lay on the beach and spend time with Momma and *you* this summer." He walked closer to the bed, placed a knee between my legs, leaned in close to kiss me, and then continued. "Second, I feel that this presentation won't be my best work because it's a rush job, but you left me no choice."

I raised my brows in question.

"Watch, read, and be quiet. You may speak when I'm finished." Griffin picked up the top poster and held it up for me to read.

"Love is putting someone else's needs before yours." —Olaf from *Frozen*

"Now, while I get that somewhere in that maybe-he's-been-tackled-too-many-times brain of yours you may *think* that breaking up with me is for the best and is putting my needs before your own, I have to remind you of something. What I *need* and what I *want* is you by my side, you big dummy. You can't put my needs before your own if my needs include having you in my life."

My nose and eyes stung but I simply nodded.

Griffin held up the next poster.

"Encourage those you love to pursue their (healthy) interests, even if your own interests lie elsewhere."—**Beauty and the Beast**

"Do you expect me to learn and like football? Basketball? Hockey? Baseball?" Griffin's rapid-fire questions had me shaking my head. "Okay. Just like I wouldn't expect you to change majors and enroll in the cosmetology program with me. I feel like this one is just so obvious it's like *duh*, but maybe you need a reminder." He dropped the poster and put his hands on my knees. "Our differences are what make us special, unique. It's okay for us to like different things. You've been harping on that from the beginning. Every time I said maybe we were just too different, you lit into me. Now it's time for you to hear the words right back."

"You were talking about our finances and families," I began.

Griff put a finger to my lips. "Different is different. You taught me that our differences don't matter. You can't change that now."

I smirked.

Griffin held up a third poster.

"But the thing that makes Woody special is that he'll never give up on you… ever. He'll be there for you, no matter what." — Andy from *Toy Story*

"We're each other's Woody. Don't you see that?

We'll never give up on each other—current stupid decision notwithstanding—we'll be there for each other. Always." Griffin's words caught in his throat and he sniffed.

"Babe, I'm sorry," I started.

"I'm not done." Griffin reached for another poster.

"Forever is a long time if you don't have someone to share it with."—Hercules

"I don't want to face forever without you." Tears began to stream down Griffin's face as he picked up his final poster.

"You mean more to me than anyone in this whole world."—Peter Pan

My heart clenched, tears overflowed, and I opened my arms to Griffin.

"Wait," Griffin croaked and held up a finger. "I need you to know, if breaking up is *really* and *truly* what you want, I'll step aside. If you don't want to be with me, if this isn't what you had hoped it would be, I won't fight you." He walked closer to the bed to stand between my legs. "But if this is just some wild notion you got, some crazy idea that I'd somehow be better off without you, then I will fight you." He punched a fist lightly against my chest while tears continued to pour. "I'll fight you because I love you. I want you. I *need* you in my life. We're better together, right?" He punched me again with no force.

I shuddered and pulled him close. "Forever better together," I mumbled against his mouth before kissing him.

EPILOGUE

Quincy

FOUR YEARS Later

I woke to a fiery heat engulfing my cock and slim fingers gripping my hips as Griffin sucked me deep to the back of his throat.

"Whoa, happy graduation day to *me*." I reached under the blankets and took hold of Griffin's hair as I threw my head back and enjoyed the pleasure his very talented mouth brought me.

Griffin grunted and let my cock fall from his mouth. "It's *my* graduation day, too." He crawled up my torso and emerged from the blankets. His hair was a mess, his lips pink and swollen, his cheeks flushed. "And I want to start the day right."

I nodded and attempted not to smile. "You're right. We should get started with a healthy breakfast."

Griffin tweaked my nipple. "I was thinking more along the lines of your dick buried in my ass until we both come so hard we see stars. *Then* we can worry about breakfast."

I glanced at the clock on the desk. "We're going to be pushing it for time."

"Are you going to refuse a graduation day morning fuck session?" Grif cocked a brow.

"Hell no. I'm just saying we may end up having to rush to get there." I propped my arms behind my head and settled in to watch the show. There were very few things I liked more than watching Griffin straddle my hips and impale himself on my dick.

A few moments later, I couldn't take it any longer. I gripped his hips and began to thrust hard and fast into his ass while Grif jacked himself. When we both exploded, Griffin leaned forward on my chest and kissed me while I wrapped my arms around him and pumped my throbbing cock gently in and out.

He whimpered into the kiss. "I'm going to be walking across the stage awkwardly today."

"And I'll enjoy every damn step you take knowing your ass is tender because of me." I licked his lips and pulled slowly from him. "I love you. But we better get a move on. Momma and Mae are probably already downstairs. Max is likely waiting at the auditorium."

Griffin and I had continued to live in campus housing all four years of college; in a strange twist of fate, we'd been allowed to stay in our suite the entire time. Overall, it was just easier to live on campus.

Closer to everything. Made getting to practices easier. Both of us had to stay on campus if we wanted to keep the meal plan that came with our scholarships. Plus, it made more sense to live rent-free on campus while saving our money until we graduated.

After today, we'd have a week to clear out of our suite.

Griffin had put down the deposit and first three months' rent on an amazing apartment we'd discovered. The location would put Grif close to his job and me almost as close to the sports management firm where I'd landed a sweet-ass position working on a team with two of the top agents in the country. I planned to observe, learn, and model myself after them in hopes of eventually getting some top-name clients of my own.

We jumped in the shower and only wasted a few moments kissing and soaping each other up. Four years of hard work was finally about to pay off. We rushed around getting dressed, fixing our hair, and gathering our robes and ridiculous-looking caps before zooming down the elevator and all but running out the door.

"It's about darn time you two showed up." Momma stood with her hands on her hips on the small patio outside our building. "Don't think I wasn't about two seconds from coming and dragging you two out by your ears. I've seen your naked butts before."

I laughed at Griffin's red cheeks and kissed him before pulling him close. "Guess we can't say she doesn't know us well." He blushed even pinker.

Griffin and I took turns hugging Momma and Aunt

Mae. The four of us had grown even closer over the last four years thanks to winter, spring, and summer trips to Florida. One of our big goals was to eventually have our own place down there, but Momma and Mae were voting for us to continue staying with them.

The four of us piled into my car and I zipped through traffic to the auditorium. Max texted to say he was saving Momma and Mae's seats.

Once we parked, Griffin and I rushed to the location we'd been assigned. The ceremony was expected to last about two hours. Grif and I had contemplated not even walking during the ceremony, but Momma got a hint of that and put her foot down. "You *will* walk across that stage and we *will* be there." End of story.

A full two hours later, Griffin and I held our graduation caps and diplomas in our hands as we made our way through the crowd to meet up with Momma, Mae, and Max.

Hugs, kisses, kind words, pictures, and a few tears took place before our entire crew headed to our next stop. We'd do a late lunch afterwards, but we had a special event to take care of first.

Two years ago, when Griffin completed cosmetology school and earned his license, he landed a job at one of the most upscale salons in our area, Classy Chic. The owner, Diane, had been a guest teacher at Grif's school and took a liking to him. She offered him a job helping with reception while he was still in school. The day he earned his license, she brought him on as her newest, and youngest, stylist. She'd been mentoring Griffin for the past two years and helping him build his client list.

Six months ago, Diane announced she was opening a second Classy Chic location and she wanted to have Griffin help her run it. He wasn't required to put in any money, but Diane wanted his input on décor and business practices. Diane was providing Grif with such an amazing opportunity.

Today was the day the new Classy Chic was being dedicated. Diane and Griffin planned it that way so Max, Mae, and Momma could all be there. A lot of Grif's friends from cosmetology school were also coming to show their support.

Classy Chic was close enough to our new apartment that Grif could walk if he wanted to. The five of us walked through the front door. Diane immediately greeted us and Griffin made introductions. I'd met Diane many times; she was quite possibly *almost* as fond of Grif as I was.

Momma and Mae exclaimed breathlessly over the beauty of the salon.

"We can thank Griffin for that. The whole interior was his idea." Diane beamed and gestured around the salon.

High, exposed ceilings, the entire front of the store was gleaming glass, worn brick walls painted a bold purple, shimmering crystal chandeliers, shining glass tables, sleek black sinks and chairs, and glinting full-length mirrors all pulled together perfectly by a sparkling fountain cascading from one wall. The look could have bordered on gaudy, but something about the way Griffin had paired the décor just worked. Perfectly.

"This looks like the type of place you'd come if you wanted to be truly taken care of," Momma gushed.

"And the type of place you'd come to spend some real money," Mae agreed with a nod. "It's absolutely gorgeous."

"We're all so proud of you, Griffin." Momma kissed Grif's cheek.

"I think all of our guests are here," Diane began. "Shall we get started?"

Champagne was poured and passed around.

Diane took Grif's hand and they stood in front of the small crowd.

"When I moved to the east coast, I never imagined my salon would do even better than my three west coast locations." Diane spread her arms wide. "Not only did Classy Chic flourish on the east coast, we've grown more than I ever expected. Bringing this kid on as staff three years ago was the beginning of a very beautiful friendship and professional relationship. Making him a staff stylist two years ago gave me the idea that Classy Chic could expand to a second location." She took Griffin's hand again. "As Classy Chic prepares to open this location, I want to thank Griffin Murphy-Sanders for being part of it as a friend, a support person, and a kick-ass stylist."

Grif blushed and kissed Diane's cheek. "Thank you, Di. This opportunity is beyond any dream I ever had when I began my journey to earn my cosmetology license *and* business degree. I have much to learn, several years of hard work before I'll even contemplate feeling successful in my field."

Diane scoffed.

"*But* the fact that you believe in me and have given me such a chance to make something of myself means the world to me. Thank you to Diane, to my family and friends, and to my boyfriend, Quincy, for supporting me, encouraging me, and standing beside me through all of this." Grif raised his glass. "I am truly blessed."

Everyone toasted and sipped their champagne and gave a small round of applause.

I cleared my throat and stepped up to stand by Griffin.

Diane winked and moved to the side.

Griffin eyed me with surprise.

I squeezed his hand. "I wanted to take a minute to congratulate Diane on the opening of her newest salon. It's absolutely gorgeous. But really, who doubted it? Anything Grif touches turns out amazing."

The small crowd chuckled.

"I also wanted to congratulate Griffin on such a crazy accomplishment. Doubling up to become a cosmetologist *and* earn your business degree was a lofty goal, but if anyone could have done it, it was you. And of course, you did it with flying colors." I pulled a paper from my pocket and turned the crowd. "Bear with me, I've got a bit of a throwback to share." I caught a glimpse of Momma and Mae with shaking hands covering their mouths. Max smirked and winked. I turned quickly to face Griffin. "G, four years ago, we wrote a little something and I'm thinking it's time for you to pay up."

Griffin rolled his eyes and laughed.

"Would you please read the text of this document?" I handed the sheet of paper to Grif.

He took the paper, shook it out a bit, cleared his throat on a chuckle and began to read.

"We the undersigned do mutually agree to enter into an intimate relationship on the date signed. By mutual agreement, if either party feels uncomfortable in the relationship or decides he wishes to back out, the relationship will immediately return to ONLY adopted brothers and best friends. There will be no weirdness or hurt feelings.

In addendum to the above stated contractual text:

*The undersigned agree that IF and WHEN an intimate, committed relationship proves successful, **Griffin Murphy-Sanders** will admit he was WRONG and should have listened to **Quincy Sanders** sooner."*

I coughed. "I'm sorry, can you read that last part again, please?"

Grif smirked as he glared good-naturedly. *"In addendum to the above stated contractual text: The undersigned agree that IF and WHEN an intimate, committed relationship proves successful, **Griffin Murphy-Sanders** will admit he was WRONG and should have listened to **Quincy Sanders** sooner."*

I cleared my throat and waited.

Griffin laughed out loud, his cheeks pink. "Fine, fine. I was wrong."

"Little louder for the people in the back." I bit my lip to keep from busting out laughing.

"I was *wrong*. Taking the next step and making our relationship more was the perfect thing to do. You were right." Griffin kissed me. "There. Happy?"

"Actually, I think you should read the rest of our contract for our guests. Just to give them the whole experience." I gestured toward the paper.

Griffin frowned but shrugged. *"In addendum to the addendum: IF and WHEN the above stated intimate and committed relationship reaches a milestone of both Griffin and Quincy graduating college, the mutually agreeing parties will entertain the prospect of making the relationship more permanent with a marriage proposal by one or the other of the undersigned."*

By the time Griffin reached the end of the contract, I'd dropped to my knee and fished a black, brushed metal wedding ring from my pocket.

Griffin turned to hand the paper back and found me on my knee. His eyes went wide and he gasped. Someone in the crowd whistled; I would place bets it was Dani.

"Griffin, from the moment that scared little boy stood in my room, to the moment two scared kids pushed their beds together, to the moment we took things to the next level," I paused and grinned with a wink and Griffin snorted. I knew we were both thinking about *which* time we took things to the next level. The moonshine and hand jobs? Our accidental kiss in the living room? Or when I finally convinced him to give us a chance.

I took his hand. "Those moments and every other moment between then and now have led us to this time and place. We've proven over the past four years that we are perfect together. We were great as brothers and best friends, but we're even better as partners. I want to spend the rest of my life loving you. Will you marry me?"

Tears streamed down Griffin's face as he nodded his head. "Yes," he croaked.

I took his hand and slipped the ring onto his finger as the crowd cheered. I pulled the matching ring from my pocket.

Griffin threw his arms around my neck and kissed me through tears and laughter.

We spent the next several moments chatting with friends and accepting congratulations. When the crowd dispersed and it was just family and Diane, Momma pulled us into a big hug.

"Pops would be so proud of you two and so happy for you." Her voice was full of tears, but strong. "He always said you two were good together." She held us tighter. "My boys have always been better together."

Griffin and I laughed through our tears and replied in unison, "Forever."

ACKNOWLEDGMENTS

It's always so hard to write this part because I'm worried I'll forget someone without meaning to.

Readers- you are the reason I write. As long as you continue reading my stories, I'll continue writing them. Thank you for your support.

Bloggers- your support, reviews, and promotion are very much appreciated. Thank you!

My author buddies- I don't know that I could keep doing this without our brainstorm sessions, laughter, road trips, meals, wine, and friendship as my support.

Thank you to my betas, editors, proofreaders, and ARC readers! Your eyes and input are beyond important to me.

Brett and Gage- as usual, I doubt you even grasp how much your support, input, and friendship mean to me. This author journey has brought many wonderful things into my life, and you both are two of the BEST! I'm blessed to call you friends.

My family and friends- thank you for your love and support, always.

ABOUT THE AUTHOR

A.D. Ellis is an Indiana girl, born and raised. She spends much of her time in central Indiana as an instructional coach/teacher in the inner city of Indianapolis, being a mom to two amazing school-aged children, and wondering how she and her husband of almost two decades have managed to not drive each other insane. A lot of her time is also devoted to phone call avoidance and her hatred of cooking.

She loves chocolate, wine, pizza, and naps along with reading and writing romance. These loves don't leave much time for housework, much to the chagrin of her husband. Who would pick cleaning the house over a nap or a good book? She uses any extra time to increase her fluency in sarcasm.

Find all of Ellis' contemporary romance and male/male romance at www.adellisauthor.com

FREE books-- sign up at bit.ly/ADEllisNews for a FREE male/female romance.

Sign up at http://www.subscribepage.com/ADEllisNewsMMRomance for a FREE male/male romance book.

ALSO BY A.D. ELLIS

The BJ Boys Series (3 books)

Something About Him Series (6 books)

His Reluctant Cowboy

What Blooms Beneath

* * *

Plus several other titles:

The Storm's Gift

Holiday Island

Devoted (a Something About Him novella)

Saving Us

Stranded Hearts (a short story)

Eli & Gage (a Something About Him short story)

* * *

A.D.'s first stories (all male/female except <u>Sawyer</u> which is male/male) are in the Torey Hope and Torey Hope: The Later Years series. Find the 8 book box set HERE

Printed in Great Britain
by Amazon

29128413R00135